CRAIG'S BOOK

By
DON WILCOX

I0541513

ARMCHAIR FICTION
PO Box 4369, Medford, Oregon   97501-0168

For more information about Armchair Books and products, visit our
website at…

www.armchairfiction.com

Or email us at…

armchairfiction@yahoo.com

AN EERIE MANSION OF MYSTERY...

Inside millionaire Hamilton Craig's mansion there were some mysterious things going on. Six beautiful girls had literally vanished into thin air inside his private office—only to reappear several days later. But where had they been? What were those strange little cards that Archie Burnette always carried around? Who was the mansion's mad scientist and what strange, fantastic experiments was he working on? Lastly, why did Hamilton Craig himself seem to have developed an obvious split personality?

Don Wilcox had one of the wildest imaginations of any sci-fi writer of his era. This thoroughly enjoyable romp is another reason why he earned the nickname, "The Mad Man, Don Wilcox."

FOR A COMPLETE SECOND NOVEL, TURN TO PAGE 153

CAST OF CHARACTERS

HAMILTON CRAIG
He had to get married within 30 days or lose his inheritance. He had six women to pick from, but they wouldn't stop disappearing!

ARCHIE BURNETTE
How could he watch over his boss' mansion when his boss couldn't even remember half of what he'd told him?

HETTY HILDRETH
What a beauty, and she had fallen hard for Archie—but she had a nasty habit of vanishing into thin air every time he kissed her!

MARCUS DRAKE
He wanted you to think he was just a kindly old gardener—but his cutting shears weren't always used for pruning.

CORNELIA
She knew the value of a dollar only too well. It landed a nice fat contract with Craig and a whole lot more—a helluva lot more.

DR. SILVERHEAD
He wasn't much to look at, old and wizened, but he was probably the most brilliant scientist on Earth—a trifle nuts, though!

WHISKEY PHIL
Too much booze was his main problem. Yet it never stopped him from conjuring up valuable information and gossip.

CHAPTER ONE
The Parade

SIX dazzlingly beautiful girls on a single float—what a parade!

To be fair about it, several floats besides Hamilton Craig's were worth a second look; the military bands were good for a thrill any day; and the passing displays of streamlined architecture topped anything the crowds had ever seen.

But parades are a pretty girl's excuse for being, no doubt—or vice versa. And this architect's passing show was no exception.

"What do youse kids do the rest of the week?" some bumpkin shouted from the sidewalk.

"Howzabout a date?" his friend joined in.

Other lads gave surprised whistles, middle-aged businessmen took in the animated scenery with approving eyes, and here and there a tottering old grandpa would suddenly shake off ten years of age as the girls threw kisses at him.

Twenty blocks of continuous waving and smiling. Then the parade was over—all but the awarding of prizes. The contest judge beamed at Hamilton Craig's perfect sextette. Their triumph was complete. They had won.

When the shouting was over and the crowds were dissolving, the judge mounted the prize float to engage the six lovely young things in a private conversation—on behalf of Craig.

"Hamilton Craig asked me to divide the prize money among you, one-sixth to each."

"But we've no right to take all the money," the girl with the snappy brown eyes protested.

"*S-s-s-sh!*" another girl broke in. "The judge knows what he's doing."

The contest judge acknowledged the compliment. "The prize money is nothing to Mr. Craig. Gather 'round, fair ones. One, two, three, four, five. Where's number six? Oh, there you are, buying an ice-cream bar. Come, young lady."

"Speakin' to me, Mistah?" Number Six asked in a soft Southern drawl. "Ah'm comin'."

The first girl, Hetty by name, was still in doubt. "Some of this money should be used to pay for the float. If we could see Mr. Craig—"

"You're not to see him," said the contest judge. "He was emphatic on that point. If you don't know Hamilton Craig—well!"

Here the contest judge stepped out of his official role long enough to throw a few sidelights upon Craig the Bachelor. Between Craig's wealth and his good looks he had been kept busy warding off aggressive females. He had been known to change his address more than once to throw followers off the trail.

"They say he turns his house into a chamber of horrors to scare away ambitious socialites," the contest judge declared. "But getting back to the point, Mr. Craig does not want to see you. Only at the last minute did someone persuade him to enter a float in the parade. I'll wager that none of you six ever met him before he chose you for this job."

Hetty glanced at her companions. "Yes, all six of us are strangers to Mr. Craig, and to each other. He just picked us up to serve in this parade."

"But we are going to stick together long enough to land a contract," said one girl who had been very eager for the prize money.

The other five girls turned to her in surprise. What was this talk about a contract?

"If you can land any kind of contract from Craig," said the contest judge, handing out the prizes, "I'm for you. Already you've got the photographers and news tattlers thinking you've been in vaudeville together somewhere. Craig could put you on Broadway if he took a notion. But for an architect he's one mysterious guy, and I figure women are his blind spot."

"We'll open his eyes," said one of the girls."

Ten minutes later the six of them were on their way to Hamilton Craig's mansion.

CORNELIA, the promoter of the contract scheme, was already talking in terms of big money. This event had been a break for her, judging from her eagerness. Hetty, carrying a small camera, snapped a close-up of her expression, thinking to entitle it, "Look out, Mr. Craig."

The celebrated bachelor architect had a number of addresses. One of his hobbies was to acquire old houses and make them over. After some trial and error, the girls arrived at an old mansion on Southwest Boulevard.

"Mah heavens! What a place!" the Southern girl exclaimed. "Ah've nevah seen a bigger haouse in Chawleston."

"And to think he has all this house to himself," another girl said. "It's a shame."

Cornelia, the contract promoter, gave out with some last minute instructions. "Remember, girls, he's shy of women. He'll probably try to close the door in our faces. We've got to take him by storm. Leave the talking to me. I'll give him a line about all the circuits we've played."

"I don't like lying to him," Hetty protested.

Genevieve, sophisticated beauty, edged in front of Cornelia haughtily as they came to the entrance.

"Oh, you want to ring the doorbell?" There was jealousy in Cornelia's tone. "You think Mr. Craig prefers platinums?"

Genevieve's answer was a cold shoulder. She rang the doorbell.

No answer.

The Southern girl, who had perched herself in the window ledge, was sure someone was inside.

"All right," said Cornelia, "we'll try once more. If they don't answer, we'll barge in."

"Please. We mustn't break moral laws." This came from a girl who had had little to say heretofore. There was deep moral conviction in her tone. "Only by righteousness can we win."

"Righteousness?" said Cornelia. "We'll talk about that later. The contract's the important thing."

Still no answer from the doorbell.

"Come on, girls," said Cornelia. But it was Genevieve who cut in ahead of her to open the door.

"Don't forget the moral laws," said the quiet one with the sensitive conscience.

"And don't forget Craig's chamber of horrors," Hetty added. She had her camera ready as they entered. If there were trapdoors or dancing skeletons, she meant to snap them.

The girls found themselves within a large oaken hallway. Clusters of little round blue lights glowed like dominoes from the paneled walls. At the farthest corner of the room was a desk with a table-lamp, where the Southern girl thought she had seen someone a moment before.

The bare walls gave back weird echoes. And the girls were chilled by the resounding of their own footsteps. They drew back into a huddle.

Cornelia suggested that someone should explore the crooked corridor beyond the desk. No one volunteered.

"But there's his room!" Hetty suddenly exclaimed. "Stay back till I get a picture of it."

THE entrance off the hallway was a half-open door in the shape of a Gothic arch. Bright new copper letters formed the words:

HAMILTON CRAIG
Private Office
DO NOT ENTER

Not much could be seen through the opening other than the pink wall beyond, brightened by late afternoon sunshine.

"Mr. Craig...Mr. Craig!" Cornelia called. Her voice faded to a whisper. "I don't think he's there. This place sounds awful empty."

"Oh, Mr. Craig!" Genevieve sang out in a saccharine tune. "Oh, Mr. Cra-a-a-aig! We've come to see you!"

There must have been electric eyes in the wall. As Genevieve walked toward the door it softly swung closed.

Both Cornelia and Genevieve fell back, but the red-haired girl named Patsy marched ahead angrily.

"Nobody's going to slam a door in my face!" Patsy tossed her head. She was in a fighting mood. She flung the door wide open.

At that instant, a thousand bars of light stabbed in from all sides of the Gothic arch. A thousand electric sparklers seemed to be going off at once. The rattle and hum were terrifying at first, and the light was blinding.

Then Patsy called back, "Come on, girls. I think he's back this way."

The straight bright bars of light continued to vibrate through the doorway, but there was still an opening in the center where Patsy had disappeared. Patsy was still calling, now from a distance. There was no terror in her voice. "Come on, we'll show him he can't scare us."

"It's just a trick," said Genevieve haughtily, and she walked through the opening within the fan of electric bars.

Cornelia followed her. Both girls disappeared.

"Wheah did they all go?" the Southern girl asked, starting forward.

"Better wait," Hetty advised, "until we see what this is all about."

"Ah nevah befo' saw a thunderstorm in a haouse."

"We have no business in the house," Hetty declared.

"We departed from the path of righteousness," said Grace, the girl with the moralistic point of view. "This thunderstorm is a warning."

"I think it's a practical joke," said Hetty, "but if they don't hurry back we had better take a chance and follow them."

The voices of the others faded in the distance. If they were still talking, the snap of electric sparks drowned them out.

As the minutes passed, Hetty and her two companions grew too curious to wait any longer. They approached the electrified opening.

"Did you see which way they went?" Hetty asked.

"As fah as mah eyes could tell," said the Southern girl, "they turned into nothing."

"They must have gone to the right," Hetty decided. "Well, here goes."

The trio filed through the electrically charged opening and, like the others, "turned into nothing."

Or, as a certain observer of the transformation afterward declared, "almost nothing."

CHAPTER TWO
Archie Swings 'Round the Block

THE single observer who took in the scene of transformation at the Gothic doorway was Archie Burnette, a young man of twenty-six who needed a job.

Archie Burnette was in Craig's private office on business, but no one knew he was there. He had come two hours before, with the purpose of fulfilling an assignment for the Overton Employment Agency. If he made good, he had been told, he might land a job with Hamilton Craig himself.

The instructions from Overton's had been brief. Archie guessed that the agent himself was mystified over the nature of this errand.

"You are to go out to Hamilton Craig's new house," the agent had said. Mr. Craig wants some more information before he moves in. The address is 7599 Southwest Boulevard. You will find a series of buildings. There used to be an old hospital in that block. The mansion that fronts on the street was the doctor's home. You're to count the rooms."

"In the mansion or the hospital?" Archie had asked.

"All the rooms. The three or four buildings on the block are all connected. Some of them are still occupied, I think. But you must walk right in and survey the whole block and list the number of rooms on every level."

And so Archie Burnette had missed the parade. He had taken a car to the suburb on the outer limits of Southwest Boulevard. He had circled the block two or three times before nerving himself to walk in at one of the brick-walled Gothic entrances.

With pencil and notebook he had followed through one room after another. Along the west side a wing of the old hospital had been converted into an apartment hotel. Off the small lobby there was a cafe a few steps below the street level. The tables were empty. At the bar three or four men were dozing over their drinks.

The attendant at the bar gave Archie the approximate floor plan, informing him which of the rooms were occupied.

"Business is bad," the bartender said. "Nobody wants to live in an old broken-down building. Look at those walls. The south wing is worse. It's vacant except for the laboratories on the second and third."

"What kind of laboratories?"

"Search me. I've never paid any attention, but I see Dr. Silverhead go by every day or two. He's one of these long-haired professors that you read about. I suppose he's happy."

Archie felt uneasy over the bartender's disclosures. It seemed that most of the tenants of these buildings were in arrears on their rent, and every reference to Dr. Silverhead heightened Archie's suspicions.

"He never pays nothin'," the bartender said, "but he's in that side of the hospital that nobody could use anyhow. When the roof falls in on him, maybe somebody will rebuild on this spot. That's why I'm holding on here. It's a damn good location."

"I'd better get over and see the doctor," said Archie.

The doors were locked, and no one would answer his knock. He passed along the windows and got what he could of the laboratory interior. The largest room on the ground floor of the south side had been an auditorium. The seats were piled up with lumber and rolls of canvas, and unopened crates of glistening scientific apparatus.

From what Archie could see of the stage, it, too, was a strange mixture of battered scenery and bright metal paraphernalia that Archie could not readily classify.

Beyond the south wing of the old hospital, Archie found his way through a passage into a courtyard. Someone had tended a garden here. In recent weeks the lawn had been mowed and apparently a new fence had been built around an old well in the center of the court. However, much of the rambling shrubbery had been neglected. He walked along the graveled paths, almost hidden from the surrounding arcades.

He found his way into the old mansion through a window. He walked softly now. Voices were echoing through the corridors that joined the laboratories.

ARCHIE preferred to avoid company. He carried a statement from the employment agency and could explain his presence if necessary. But the bartender had given him a suspicion toward the scientist who occupied these premises.

The voices soon were out of hearing.

Each new room he entered greeted him with a glow of electric lights. Obviously, some recent electric wiring had been done in this place. Electric eyes were turning on these lights whenever he crossed a threshold.

Now he entered a corner chamber where the light of the afternoon sun brightened the pink walls. The door ahead was half opened. He could see a sign on it: "Hamilton Craig-Private Office-Do Not Enter."

Here for the first time he had discovered something familiar. But the room itself showed no signs of being occupied by Craig. Dusty linen covers were over the furniture. The floor had not been swept. The only foot tracks in the dust were those near the door. Obviously, these copper letters had been nailed on within the last day or two.

But there was something more that caught Archie's curiosity. The Gothic arch of the doorway itself was studded with a row of tiny copper points, like a string of sharp-pointed beads. A well-insulated wire was attached to the lower end of this border of points.

Archie frowned and backed away. The automatic lighting of rooms had put him on his guard.

He was debating how to get out of Craig's private office without crossing that threshold when he heard the chatter of female voices in the room beyond.

Archie ducked back into an alcove. He listened. From the hallway of soft blue lights these girls were daring each other to enter this private office.

"Ye gods!" Archie thought. "If they come in here looking for Craig and find me—" Archie's thoughts turned a series of flip-flops. It would be funny, he thought, to pose as Craig. If he only had a little more nerve—but things like that only happened in plays. He edged back into the next room and vowed he would not emerge no matter what happened.

Then before his eyes the strangest, most unbelievable things occurred.

First of all, the door seemed to close by itself.

Next, someone flung it open, and he saw a beautiful red-haired girl come through. Instantly there was a shower of electrical sparks from the sides of the doorway. To Archie it was like a thousand tracer bullets shooting straight at the girl.

But she came on and turned to call to the others. She was still calling *when she vanished in thin air.*

A second and a third girl followed. The brilliant shower of electrical sparks threatened them as they passed through the doorway. And yet Archie thought that they were not touched, for after they were safely within the room he could see an open space in the center of the door framed by the cracking little bolts of lightning.

The light was blinding, and Archie was reluctant to trust his eyes; but what he seemed to see now was a little white card fluttering in the air. It drifted across a table and dropped down upon the dusty linen cover.

Within the next two or three minutes a total of six different girls had entered the room through the barrage of electrical vibrations, and all of them, if Archie could believe his eyes, had turned invisible.

Six girls disappeared—six white cards materialized out of thin air and fluttered down to the table.

Everything was perfectly silent except for the beating of Archie's heart. He could not catch his breath. In fact, he was under a nightmare paralysis. The electrical spray was still humming and snapping dangerously, and he had momentary visions of being extinguished by it.

Suddenly there were footsteps from the room beyond. The fan of electrical bars snapped off. A tall, straight man walked in briskly—*Craig himself.*

Before Archie could break out of his frozen state, Hamilton Craig picked up the six white cards, fitted them into a little leather-backed book, pocketed it and strode out.

CHAPTER THREE
Archie Becomes a Bookkeeper

HEEDLESS of the dangerous door, Archie ran after the disappearing figure of Craig. He raced across the blue-lighted hallway, and followed through a luxurious dining room beyond. There he stopped, confused as to which of several doors Craig had taken.

The pursuit was a hopeless one. With a quickening sense of responsibility he added these rooms to his notebook charts. He would reconstruct the rest by guess. It was high time to get back to the Overton Employment office, by taxi.

The agent at Overton's greeted Archie with a not too friendly, "Well, it's about time. Five minutes more and we would have been closed. Go back to Booth Seven. Craig is waiting."

"Craig?" Archie gulped.

A moment later Archie was shaking hands with Hamilton Craig himself, and the slender, stern-looking businessman was scrutinizing him with sharp black eyes.

"You sure do get around, Mr. Craig," Archie mumbled.

"Sit down, Mr. Burnette, we haven't much time to talk."

Archie was skeptical. What sort of man was this? Was he not carrying six "magic cards" in his pocket? The weird events of the past hour were shooting through Archie's brain like skyrockets. How could this handsome, black-mustached man sit there so coolly, fingering his checkbook with such a steady hand?

Archie presented his sketchy notebook report of the rooms and buildings he had surveyed. He apologized for the lack of accuracy.

"I didn't go through the whole house on the east. I was sort of confused. After what happened—"

"Don't mention it," said Craig. "You made a good beginning. I can use you. I have looked over your employment record. You seem to be resourceful. I think you have about the right amount of nerve. It wouldn't do to be too foolhardy."

This was a dubious compliment, Archie thought. Also, it implied something ominous regarding the job.

Craig made out a check and passed it over. "Here's an advance. You start at once. If you stick, the salary will be fifty a week."

"I'll be ready to go to work tomorrow."

"You start this evening. I want you to go back to the Southwest Boulevard mansion and pick up a book."

Archie frowned. He tapped the folded check on the table. "Pardon me, Mr. Craig, but just what sort of work is this?"

"You applied for a bookkeeper's position, didn't you? Well, that's it. You are to be my bookkeeper. I will dignify you with the title of my personal secretary, sergeant-at-arms and night watchman. How's that?"

"It sure sounds like a steady job. When will I ever have time for dates with my girl friends?"

"You have girl friends?" Craig was very serious.

"If I don't have now, I will have as soon as I start earning."

Craig gave a satisfied smile. "That's fine. I've picked the right man, I'm sure. You will have a date every night."

Archie rose, feeling that he ought to be indignant. In the movies he had seen, a man like himself would have torn up the check and said, "What do you think I am—a gigolo?"

IN THE moment of indecision Craig came to the rescue. "You are right. Money isn't everything. Your personal honor is involved. We'll make the salary seventy-five."

"Thank you," said Archie weakly. He took the new check.

"Now listen carefully," said Craig. "My lawyer has warned me that I must get married within thirty days. Either that, or lose an empire of apartment buildings. An inheritance clause, you understand. My uncle Jimpson had tricky notions."

"Thirty days to get married in…" Archie regarded the celebrated bachelor with awe. "Gosh…who's the lucky lady?"

"I haven't the slightest idea. I have been too busy to get acquainted with any women. In fact, I have had to take severe measures to protect myself. So let's be frank about it, girls make me nervous."

"Well, of course, too many girls—" Archie was trying to be sympathetic.

"You see," Craig continued, "a man of wealth like myself can never be sure that girls aren't deceiving him. But I have hit upon an ideal scheme for getting acquainted. I have just acquired six prospective wives."

"Six…" Archie gulped. Wasn't that the number of girls that had come through the electrified door?

"Six—and what a bunch! Regular *cards* from what I have seen of them." Craig gave a little contented laugh. "But the way I'm arranging things I'll be able to keep my distance.

You will help me discover which is the—shall I say, least objectionable one. So for the present you are to make no other dates."

"Well, I will take their addresses," said Archie dubiously.

"That won't be necessary. Your bookkeeping procedure will make it very easy for you to keep tab on them. Their headquarters will be my own mansion on Southwest Boulevard."

Archie gave a low whistle. The thought of six rival girls staying together in the same house sounded like trouble aplenty.

Craig rose. "That's all. You're to begin by going back to the mansion at once. I want you to pick up a book for me. You will find it in the desk in the corner of the oak paneled reception room. Here's a key.

"It's a little brown leather-backed book. Be sure the book is snapped shut. I don't want you to lose anything out of it. You see it contains six cards—"

"Yes, I know."

"Oh, you know..." Craig's penetrating eyes were searching Archie curiously. "Well, then, you know something about your bookkeeping job, don't you?"

Archie stammered, "I—er—I was in the next room when you came into your private office and gathered up the cards."

"All right." Craig smiled mysteriously. "Take the book home with you. Report to me at my downtown office tomorrow at nine. If time weighs on your hands between now and then, get out the cards and play a game of solitaire."

CHAPTER FOUR
Archie Picks Up a Card

THE doctors' mansion and hospital buildings had been dreary and forbidding in the daytime; by darkness they presented a weird and fearsome aspect. Archie circled the block slowly.

He chided himself. There was nothing to be afraid of. He had only to enter the east mansion door, pick up the book and leave. What difference should it make that the doctor in the south wing had drawn all the blinds, or that mysterious men were drifting along these sidewalks?

Archie sauntered up the steps. The dank smell of aging brick walls greeted him as he opened the door. The little dominoes of blue lights were glowing. His footfalls echoed through the hall rooms. He wasted not a step.

The desk drawer was locked, all right. He turned the key, opened the drawer. Yes, the little brown book was there. If Archie was surprised, it was because he remembered the haste with which Craig must have crossed this room a few hours earlier.

Archie recalled the details distinctly. He had not seen Craig pass through this room, but he had seen that mysterious gentleman thrust the book into his pocket and make his exit from his private office into this room. And by the time Archie had gathered up presence of mind to follow him, Hamilton Craig's footsteps had clattered on into the big dining room and beyond.

Archie could hardly believe that Craig had had time to stop and deposit the book and lock the drawer in passing. Much less had he the time to make a return trip before his appearance at the employment office.

"The guy must be a screwball," Archie thought, but that didn't help much. Here was the book, and his orders were to take it.

He opened it and counted the white cards. Six of them. He held them up to the light, one after another.

"Well, I'll be damned! They are nothing but plain white paper cards."

He packed five of them back into the leather folder. He bent down to pick up the one that had dropped to the floor. It slid along the floor just out of his grasp.

He glanced about. If there was a draft of air, he could not detect it. But now the card was floating upward. The sight sent chills tingling to his fingertips. He had better get it back into the book and get out of here.

He made a grab for it, but it was *gone*.

Then it happened. Before his eyes there appeared some filmy ectoplasm. Archie could not call it anything else because he did not believe in ghosts. The shadowy substance immediately filled out into something very tangible, not to mention beautiful.

"Well, hello," said Archie, more than a little flabbergasted. "You're one of Craig's girls—"

"I beg your pardon…" The girl who had materialized before Archie's eyes was a shapely brunette, garbed in the colorful Chinese costume she had worn in the architect's parade float. There was a little anger in her snappy brown eyes. But Archie thought she was more bewildered than angry.

As for himself, Archie was just a bit bowled over. "Gosh…Craig can pick 'em!"

"Oh…Craig…that's where I am. I had forgotten. Well, thank goodness I'm out of that party. Which way do I—"

She turned and started for the door.

"Wait. Don't hurry off. You must meet Craig."

The girl hesitated. A chance to meet Hamilton Craig was something no girl could ignore.

"I ought to get home. I'm a working girl, you know, and after all, I don't even know who you are."

"Allow me to present myself, Archie Burnette, Mr. Craig's secretary."

ARCHIE made a grandiose gesture. To him this situation was something right out of the movies. He could not let this girl get away without finding out where she came from. And besides, he had his obligations to Craig.

"All right, I'm Hetty Hildreth," the girl said, "and you may tell Mr. Craig I paid my respects."

"Wait. Where do you work?"

"At the big photographers' supply house on Twelfth and Main. I'm their top saleslady, if I do say so myself. You see I always carry a camera. There!"

Before Archie could say whether he liked it or not, she had taken a flashlight picture of him. But Archie liked it. He liked everything about this girl. However, he could think of only one good reason for detaining her.

"I'll call Mr. Craig at once if you'll just wait."

The girl agreed, reluctantly. She could not imagine where the time had gone. She seemed to have been asleep, she said. The last thing she remembered was entering Craig's private office with several of the girls, and she felt terrible over having intruded.

While Hetty Hildreth waited, Archie retreated into the dining room and looked around for a telephone. He might have had better luck in Craig's private office, but he did not want to chance that doorway. What he needed most of all was a minute to collect his thoughts.

"I don't dare let her get away," he said to himself. "She's one of Craig's six cards. I wish I could somehow put her back in the pack."

There were no telephones in the dining room or any of the three rooms adjoining it. Archie kept mumbling to himself. What would Craig want him to do? There ought to be a book of instructions with this job.

"Who's that?" Archie stepped out into the corridor. Three men were coming down the passage from another building. The tall man in the center was none other than Craig himself. His lips twisted beneath his black mustache. He was puffing a cigarette. There was no friendly light in his eyes for Archie.

"Wait a minute, fellows," he muttered to the two men with him. Then he said to Archie, "What's going on here?"

"Mr. Craig, I—you never told me you would be down here, too."

"Didn't I? That's too bad. What are you doing?"

"I got the book, like you told me."

"Oh…I see," said Craig, looking back at his companions who were waiting impatiently. "Well, you had better get out. It's time this place was closed up for the night."

"But one of the girls is here—I mean—it happened when one of the cards fell out. I think you ought to meet her."

"No time now. Besides, I met her when I made up the float. Come along; we are closing up."

Craig and his two companions hurried on, and the last Archie heard was a final echo of the same advice.

THIS conversation had taken him into the oak-paneled reception room, where Hetty Hildreth had made herself as obscure as possible. He turned to her apologetically. He guessed there was no time for sociability this evening.

"I should think not," Hetty gasped. "They flew through like an express train. I was tempted to take their pictures, but—"

"Not afraid of my boss, are you?"

"No, but those other two fellows—they looked like gangsters."

Archie laughed. "I guess Craig can take care of himself. Look—this is kind of funny. There's no way to lock this door. I'll tell Craig about that the first thing tomorrow."

They started down the steps, and Archie searched the street for a taxi. Somehow he knew it was wrong, but he could not think of any way out. He would take this girl home.

But before a taxi came along he found another pretext for delay. A well dressed, heavy-jowled man had just passed, and Archie retained an image of a brutal face, a monocle and a white bow tie. Now he could see that the man was ascending the steps to the mansion.

"Now who could that be?"

"Didn't you say you were Craig's secretary?" Hetty asked. She seemed to be teasing him. "I'd think you'd know the house guests."

"I'm just starting," said Archie. "Seems as if Craig keeps open house. If you don't mind, I'll park you at this corner drugstore while I go back and investigate."

"I won't be parked," said Hetty, "but I'll go back with you. From the looks of things it must be a town meeting."

Archie saw that she was referring to another man who had just crossed to the yard from a parked car. He, too, was ascending the steps of the huge brick house.

"Of course, if you would rather put me in a taxi and send me home alone, it's quite all right."

"I'd rather have you come along," Archie said, and wondering if he was revealing cowardice on his part, he added, "I mean you're being a mighty good sport to go adventuring with me this time of night."

"You don't know me," said Hetty. "I'm always on the lookout for good camera subjects. That bulldog with the white tie and the monocle—can't you imagine me, coming into the store with his picture?"

"You're sure you're not afraid? This place is a haunted house if I ever saw one."

"I shouldn't be afraid as long as I'm with you. If you're Craig's secretary, it's your business to know what's going on."

At the top of the steps Archie glanced back to make sure no one else was coming. Only two cars were parked between the streetlights. Probably this was the lonesomest block in all the city.

Hetty walked in silently. Archie followed, and he was careful to close the door noiselessly.

CHAPTER FIVE
Three Camera Subjects

IN THE reception room of the mansion the blue lights burned continuously. For a few rooms beyond the lights had gone on, one after another, as each of the men had crossed into the hospital building.

Archie had no intention of actually eavesdropping when he and Hetty set out to follow this series of lights. If he had considered it essential to keep his presence a secret, he would have searched for some master switch to cut off all these electric eyes that flashed lights on automatically.

But as he and Hetty came within earshot of the conference between the two men, they decided it would be wise not to intrude. The voices were discussing a matter that was evidently outside the letter of the law.

"My Gosh! They sound like a crime ring..." Archie whispered, as Hetty grabbed his arm nervously.

"We'd better get out," the girl whispered. "It's some kind of a business secret."

But she clung to Archie's arm and they continued to listen. Gradually they edged closer. Since entering the hospital building they had been in almost total darkness. Luckily the system of automatic lighting had been left behind. But it was odd, Archie thought, that these two men dared to meet in a lighted room and discuss their affairs in unguarded tones.

Presently Archie and Hetty found their way into a dark room in which furniture had been stored. Perhaps it had been a kitchen at one time, for there was a service window. A thin line of light filtered in from the adjoining conference room.

"There's our man with the monocle," Hetty whispered.

Archie tapped her hand as if warning her not to breathe. Together they peered through the narrow opening beneath the window, resting their arms in the deep dust on the ledge.

The conference room was lighted by a single desk lamp. The man in the swivel chair appeared to be waiting while his client read some papers.

The client, if such he was, was an elderly gentleman with an ivory-tinted walrus mustache, the ends of which trembled, betraying his nervousness as he peered at the paper.

"What a show," Hetty whispered breathlessly. "What I wouldn't give for a movie camera."

Archie knew she was scared, though. He was putting on the bravery act, holding her hand to keep her from trembling. And yet he tended to shudder whenever he looked at the thick, brutal face of the man in the swivel chair.

With puffy fingers this thickset person tapped his monocle on the desktop. He tossed his head back and forth. His right eyebrow went up and his left one clamped down tighter as he eyed his prospect.

"If there's anything you don't understand," said the thickset man, adjusting his monocle, "Dr. Silverhead will be here in a few minutes."

He consulted his watch. He drew an orchid-colored cigarette holder from his pocket and lit a cigarette. His client was a slow reader.

"I had better call Dr. Silverhead to be sure," the thickset man continued. "He's very absent-minded. He may have forgotten."

There was no answer to the telephone call. The client looked up.

"Didn't you get him, Mr. Drake?"

"He must be on his way up. Is there any question about that contract, Mr. Rickenthorp?"

"I—I think not."

THE man with the walrus mustache seemed unsure of himself. "You are sure that everything will be all right, Mr. Drake?"

"Now, Mr. Rickenthorp, don't be foolish," said the thickset man, puffing confidently. "You have been contacted in three previous interviews. You have been assured that many big men are investing in this experiment. You were advised not to come for the fourth interview unless you were ready to lay the money on the line."

"I'm ready," said Mr. Rickenthorp, weakly. "If this works out, it will pay bigger than anything I have ever tried."

"It will work out, Mr. Rickenthorp. It may take time and, as you understand, some human sacrifice will be involved."

The fragile old gentleman managed a laugh. "I guess we can stand that." He counted out a number of bills.

Drake handed his client a fountain pen. "Before I touch the money, you must sign, and have I called your attention to this particular clause?"

"I have it practically memorized," said Rickenthorp. He read it over aloud: " 'My complete endorsement of this plan is denoted, first, by my investment, and secondly, by my fullest approval of whatever measures the experimenter sees fit to take, even though the sacrifice of human lives may be necessitated.' "

With trembling hand the old gentleman signed.

Footsteps could be heard from down the corridor. Drake looked up sharply. As soon as the hall lights came on he seemed to be satisfied.

"It's Dr. Silverhead. He didn't forget, after all."

From their hiding place, Archie and Hetty could see the white-haired newcomer as he tottered into the conference room. So this was Dr. Silverhead. A wizened old man, with crisp white mustaches and goatee, and watery eyes that seemed to be seeing visions.

The doctor was absent-minded indeed. He evidently knew he had come to meet a client. It was Drake that he approached with his greeting, until the former apprised him of his mistake.

"It is Mr. Rickenthorp you have come to meet," Drake said. "Mr. Rickenthorp has just signed our agreement."

The doctor shook hands with the walrus-mustached man, but did not bother to look at him. The ceiling seemed to be more attractive to the doctor, who kept up an incessant mumbling about his own troubles.

"I have been calling everywhere to try to get some lenses. No place is open this time of day. It is an outrage. If I were making lenses I would try to give service to the most important people. There ought to be more lens-makers. I broke the one good lens I had. Yes, I may be driven to do it myself. I have made other professional equipment. Is there any reason why I could not make lenses?"

"Of course you could make them," said Drake, "but now I want you to say a word to Mr. Rickenthorp. He is ready for the experiment."

The doctor was profoundly affected by this announcement. He paced back and forth in front of the client, patted him on the shoulder and shook him by the wrist.

"So you are going to help us out. That's fine—fine. I admire your courage, your spirit of sacrifice."

"What is this?" The walrus-mustached man was nonplussed. "Oh, you mean I get to watch you perform something."

"Precisely," said the doctor jubilantly, "you will see it from the inside. You are going to be the experiment yourself."

"Oh, no, not me! I came here as an investor."

Drake looked down his cigarette holder, fixed his monocle and drew a revolver out of his pocket. He spoke brusquely.

"Don't start backing out. You have just signed this document. That proves you are willing to spend lives in this cause. All right, the next life on the program happens to be yours."

CHAPTER SIX
Trail of Shadows

BECAUSE of Hetty, Archie had made a show of bravery in plunging blindly into this eavesdropping situation. Hetty had believed in him. Her confidence gave him courage.

Now he studied the hard, cruel eyes of Drake and knew that this treacherous swindler meant business. No one would dare play this game and risk letting a client get away. The walrus-mustached man was in for it.

The girl whispered, "What are we going to do?"

"Hold back. Follow them if they march him away. If it wasn't for those darned lights—"

"I've got to get this." Hetty brought the camera up to the ledge and pointed it through the narrow aperture. The three men inside were standing like statues. It was the victim's move, but he was too astonished to do more than tremble.

Archie had momentary visions of a flashlight bulb explosion and the effect it would have upon this tense deadlock. He pressed Hetty's hand.

"Don't do it. That fellow Drake is desperate. He'll start shooting at this service window and ask questions afterwards."

"Don't worry," Hetty whispered. "Everything's okay."

A moment later, when the three camera subjects broke out of their freeze, Hetty removed the camera. Then Archie knew she had taken a bulb exposure.

In the conference room, the victim yielded ground. As he edged toward the door, Drake followed him with the gun on a level with his heart. Meanwhile, Dr. Silverhead went on with his glib chatter. The gunplay was of secondary importance to him. He was talking about experiments and his eagerness to try certain new lenses. He was even thanking the dazed Mr. Rickenthorp for his readiness to cooperate.

As the three of them made their way through the door, Archie lost any hope that Rickenthorp might try to break and run. In this moment of danger he was without resources.

"They've got him," Archie whispered. "He wouldn't run out if his own house was on fire."

"Where you going?" the girl asked.

"After them. You stay back. If you don't hear from me within five minutes, call the police."

Archie crept to the door. He ran his hand over the dusty furniture in search of a weapon. Off the top of a heap he took a folding chair.

"Careful," Hetty whispered. "They are coming back."

She waited with him beside the door just inside the deep shadows. The snarling voice of Drake could be heard as he re-entered the next room.

"Don't move, Rickenthorp—I'll be right with you."

The gunman's heavy tread sounded across the conference room floor. He rummaged through the desk and gathered up some papers. The frightened Rickenthorp had found his voice and was beginning to rant.

"This is an outrage," he cried, "and you won't get away with it. If you would only sit down and talk it over sensibly I can make it worth your while to cancel the contract."

Drake gave a cynical laugh.

"This deal is too big to be bought off with cash. Haven't we already told you that Dr. Silverhead is going to revolutionize his profession? What he needs is cooperation from farsighted business men like yourself—Mr. Buddy Rickenthorp. All right, now you can march down and help the doctor put his theories into practice."

This time Drake snapped off the light over the conference desk. Only the dim yellow light halfway down the corridor was burning.

AS THE three men moved along, their jumping shadows retreated from the doorway where Archie and Hetty waited. Archie relaxed his grip on the folding chair. It seemed that the moment for action had passed him by.

"What will they do to him?" Hetty whispered tensely.

"They won't let him out alive, you can be sure of that. The fool! He let himself in for it, but all the same—"

"We've got to do something."

Archie rummaged through the shelves. There were all sorts of kitchen equipment in the place. He grabbed a handful of heavy china teacups. He picked up a butcher knife, but his own boldness startled him. He dropped it.

All the way down the hall he kept wishing he could change his armful of weapons for a good solid baseball bat.

Hetty was following him, warning him to come back. How could he dare take such a desperate chance? He knew the answer to that. It was because he was seeing himself in her eyes—bold, foolhardy.

The trio had disappeared, and the corridor light had gone off when they rounded the corner. Now their footsteps were sounding down a stairway, and the only light was that wafting up from the foot of the staircase. Archie could gauge their progress by the bouncing shadows. If he was swift enough, this was his opportunity. He was sprinting almost noiselessly.

He reached the head of the stairs, folding chair in one arm, teacups in the other. Down the creaky old stairs the solemn trio was marching. They had heard nothing.

With utmost care he placed the folding chair at one side of the top step and three of the teacups at the other.

Before he went into action, he crept down to the third or fourth step. Then his good right arm did its stuff. In rapid succession—*one, two, three*—he hurled the teacups straight at the electric light bulb.

The instant the missiles began whirring through the air there were growls of surprise from Drake and his prisoner.

But the last aim was true, and before Drake could turn, the light bulb was shattered. Archie grabbed up the chair.

The darkness wasn't complete. A dim light filtered up from the floor below. It gave Archie an advantage he had not counted on. As he leaped down the stairs swinging the folding chair over his head, he got a perfect silhouette of Drake coming up with his gun-arm ready.

Crash!

The folding chair landed like a ton of bricks. Drake went down with a breathy *oooof* like a punctured balloon. Then he and Archie were rolling down the stairs together, and Archie was throwing punches as fast and furious as he could. By the time they hit the floor below, there were four of them in the scramble.

One of them, however, was out for the count, and that one was Drake.

Over the excited mumbling of Dr. Silverhead and the grunts of consternation from Rickenthorp, Archie shouted. He shouted with such excitement in his voice that he hardly knew himself.

"Now get out, you fool, if you've got any sense! This is your chance! Beat it!"

With that, Archie went bounding up the steps, three at a time, hesitating only to pick up the gun that had dropped on the stairs.

A few minutes later he and Hetty were crossing the city in a taxi.

Archie would never forget that ride. It seemed that the beautiful girl beside him could not get her breath. She kept saying, "How did you do it? Gee, I didn't think you could get away with it. Honest, I never saw anything like it."

"Could you even see what happened?"

"First I saw the gunman. Then, when the light went out I just knew he'd be shooting you full of holes. But I had to look anyway. And I was just in time to see you jump down the steps swinging that chair over your head. Honest, Archie, I never saw anything like it."

Archie slipped his arm around her and looked into her eyes intently.

"Believe me, I wouldn't have done it if you hadn't been there." As he said it, Archie knew that he was not kidding this girl. He had been a hero because of her. Without her he might have played the coward. It all added up to something pretty important, and Archie knew it. She had been a good sport to stick with him, and he had fallen hard.

Then he was trying to kiss her, and she was suddenly remembering that they had not known each other before this evening.

"You're a fast worker, Archie, but I think you're just a little excited over all that's happened."

"I know I am," he admitted, "but the evening would not be complete if I didn't kiss you goodnight."

Then they were at the door of her apartment house, and she was in his arms and he was claiming his kiss.

Kisses are known to have curious effects upon beautiful young ladies, but what happened then was more than Archie anticipated. The girl did not melt into his arms—she melted out of them! In fact, she melted out of existence, and left Archie standing there, staring.

All he saw was a white paper card floating down to the steps. He picked it up, filed it away in Craig's book, sent the taxi on its way and walked home.

CHAPTER SEVEN
Cornelia

AT NINE in the morning the events of the previous night seemed a dream, yes—a nightmare. Archie waited in the reception room on the twenty-first floor of a downtown building. There were no forbidding signs on the door of Hamilton Craig, Architect, but the door was locked.

Archie was in the process of magnifying his fears over the walkout of Craig and the two strangers of the previous night, when Craig himself strode into the reception room.

"Good morning, Burnette. I see you're right on the dot." Craig's voice was hearty. He was like a man with no troubles in the world.

Archie followed him into the office. The bad news had just as well be broken at once.

"Mr. Craig, what the devil goes on out there on Southwest Boulevard? Are you harboring a gang of racketeers or something?"

Craig laughed lightly. He sat down at his desk and locked his hands back of his head. "The whole block was a pretty bad mess," he admitted, "but I didn't have time to straighten things up." He began to sort through some charts. "You see I'm making plans."

"But if the underworld is going to trespass on your premises—"

"I guess it isn't quite that bad," said Craig. "Of course, after the windows of a building are broken out, it's hard to tell what riffraff may come in. What did you see that aroused your suspicions?"

"Plenty," said Archie. He drew his chair closer to the desk. "After you and those two men passed me, the girl and I started out, like you told us to. And then—"

"Hold on," Craig interrupted, "what girl was this?"

"You know. The one I wanted you to stop and meet. Her name's Hetty Hildreth."

"Oh, yes." Craig gazed up at the ceiling. "She was one of the parade girls. Tell me about her. Did you like her?"

"But this crime racket, Mr. Craig."

"Tell me about the girl."

Archie drew a long breath. He was not sure where to begin. "Gosh, if I could only recite poetry—well, to begin with, she's one swell gal."

Archie found himself growing a bit dreamy as he recited the virtues of Hetty, and before he knew it he was sure he had waxed much too enthusiastic. Craig's eyes were glowing. "But you might not fall for her like I did," Archie said. His instinct told him it was time to pull his punches.

"She sounds interesting."

"You might not care for her. I doubt if you would. She's pretty young—"

"I'd like to meet her. Right away. Do you think it could be arranged?"

Archie fumbled for an answer.

"Well—er—it was sorta strange the way I happened onto her."

Craig was eyeing the little leather book in Archie's pocket.

"No stalling, Burnette. You had just as well get used to this convenience of having beautiful girls at our beck and call. Notice I said *our*. I'll bet Hetty Hildreth would be delighted to have lunch with the two of us."

ARCHIE snapped open the book cover. He was sure that the last of the six cards was the one he wanted, and his hands were not nervous. Nevertheless, as he grabbed for it, a different card dropped out toward the floor.

It barely touched the carpet. Then, as if by magic, it rose to the level of the table and vanished.

"Ah!" said Craig. "You are becoming accustomed to this clever little gadget."

"It's the wrong one," Archie gasped. "It isn't Het—"

Craig hushed him with a gesture. Out of the air had come a steamy little cloud, which presently materialized into a new girl. She was slender, blonde, as beautiful as something out of Hollywood—beautiful in a different way from Hetty, Archie thought. She was still wearing her parade costume.

To Archie the sudden appearance of a beautiful girl was always something of a shock, whether she dropped out of a cloud or merely came around a corner. But he noticed that this young lady wasted only one look on him. Thereafter her eyes were fastened upon Hamilton Craig.

"This is a pleasure, Mr. Craig," she was saying, offering a drooping hand to the handsome architect. "Just call me Cornelia."

"I remember you distinctly," Craig nodded. He, too, was a little confused at having his luncheon plans upset.

"I came to see you on behalf of the six of us."

Cornelia accepted Archie's chair without acknowledging the courtesy. "I would have been here sooner, but as I walked into your private office some practical joker took advantage of me. Now, what we have in mind—we six girls who won the contest for you—is to see if you would like to have us appear in a show. As an advertising stunt I mean. You could call us the Six Craig Girls or—"

"If you'll excuse us," Craig broke in, "I'll talk with you in just a few minutes. You'll find a chair in the waiting room."

"Why...of course, Mr. Craig." Cornelia glanced at the door apprehensively. "This isn't another one of those electric things, is it? Well, I'll be waiting for you, but I warn you I'm going to land a contract, Mr. Craig."

Craig made an effort to smile politely. He closed the door behind her, and mopping his forehead turned to Archie.

"It appears that your day's work is cut out for you. Get acquainted with her. Report to me later. I'm a pretty busy man myself. Now what about this underworld business? I hope it didn't have anything to do with the old doctor who occupies the south wing of the hospital."

Archie launched into a complete account of his eavesdropping escapade.

Craig took it all in with intense interest. Then he went over the details to be sure he had missed nothing.

"Evidently I should not have allowed my two friends to lead me away," he said. "Was I—er—drunk? Never mind. The trouble lies much deeper than that."

"Seems to me the first thing you need is a good lock on every door," Archie commented.

"Right. And we'll get those broken windows boarded up. I'll make a note of it. The carpenters will be on the job today. As for the doctor, he's an enigma. I suggest you go in and get acquainted with him. Tell him you're working for me. Ask him about his experiments."

Archie tried to imagine himself meeting the doctor after what had occurred last night.

"Are you going to be there, Mr. Craig?"

Craig shot a quick, questioning glance in Archie's direction. "That's something else I meant to warn you about. *I am completely unpredictable.* You must not be surprised at my comings and goings. And you are never to stop me for any questions at the mansion. You and I will carry on our discussions here in private. That's all, Burnette."

"Then you are not going to do anything about Drake?"

"That's not your worry. Drake is the doctor's stooge. And the authorities in Southwest Boulevard know all about the doctor. They consider him harmless."

Archie had his doubts. In the waiting room he tried to work out some plan of action.

But a few minutes later he found that the planning was out of his hands. Craig had arranged for him to take Cornelia to dinner, and after that there would be a round of the smartest shows and nightclubs.

"But I must have some clothes," Cornelia said, "and I promised Mr. Craig I would be a good little girl and go out with you if you would buy me some things."

"What sort of things?"

"Just a party dress and some new slippers and things. You don't mind, do you, Archie?" She smiled at him sweetly. "Mr. Craig tells me you're getting a handsome salary."

CHAPTER EIGHT
Marcus Drake Has a Headache

ARCHIE lost Cornelia that afternoon at the perfume counter. He escaped while most of his first week's salary was still intact.

For his freedom he could thank one Carlo Verrazzano, a huge mountain of a man, who resembled a musician, and was discovered in the midst of a verbal rhapsody regarding his celebrated achievements in the fine arts of selling perfume.

Verrazzano's striking appearance was enhanced by a wealth of black hair that hung to his shoulders, plus a trimmed black mustache and a beard. No radio announcer ever advertised a lady's perfumes with any more enthusiasm than the rhapsodic Signor Verrazzano.

When this unique salesman began talking in terms of ten-thousand-dollar orders for millionaire customers, Cornelia edged in front of the cluster of listeners to catch his eye. Soon she was buying perfume and accepting the most flattering remarks from the salesman. By the time the other customers were leaving, she was one of his oldest and dearest friends.

The last Archie heard of the conversation she was saying, "But I'm sure I could cancel my other dinner engagement for you, Signor Verrazzano."

Archie caught his cue, gave her a farewell wave, and scrammed.

On his way to the mansion Archie was sorely tempted to open the little brown leather book. If he could only be sure of getting Hetty before another Cornelia jumped out—but his instinct for self-preservation told him not to risk it.

"If Craig wants to fire me for losing Cornelia," he thought, "let him do his worst. I ought to be twins for this job—no, sextuplets."

His plan of action was well laid by the time he reached 7599 Southwest Boulevard. Craig had told him to strike up an acquaintance with Dr. Silverhead. All right, he would ratchet up his courage and face the doctor.

Had Archie known more of the inside situation that he had glimpsed the previous evening, he would have been even more skeptical about making a social call. The doctor and his agent, Mr. Drake, were in no mood to receive guests

WHEN Marcus M. Drake caught the blow of the folding chair on the top of his head, he saw a whole galaxy of stars, with several spiral nebulas thrown in, and instantly one of these had engulfed him.

He did not know that he rolled to the bottom of the stairs or that some young man was hammering him with fists. Nor did he realize that the doctor stomped around in great agitation long after the anonymous assailant and the walrus-mustached victim had gone their separate ways.

After an hour or more, Drake awoke to the sound of his own groanings. He opened his eyes to receive the dim light of the second floor corridor.

With consciousness came a surge of anger. There was the absentminded doctor, pacing up and down, tapping his pencil on the wall, talking to himself.

"If I hadn't broken that lens," the doctor was saying, shaking his white goatee in great distress, "everything would be all right. But there will be another lens like that. There must be. As soon as Drake wakes up I'll have him order some equipment. I'll start at once—"

"Stop your damned mumbling," Drake growled, coming up on one elbow. "What happened? Who struck me? Where did they go?"

"I was just thinking, Drake, I'll have you order some—"

"Shut up and help me get up…"

Dr. Silverhead was all but impervious to Drake's ill humors. However, he made a show of offering a hand to Drake as the latter groped back toward the stairway on all fours and brought himself up to a sitting position.

Drake turned and stared up into the darkness. His repeated demands as to who his assailants were and where they had gone were lost on the doctor.

"I can't fathom it, Drake. Why do all of our subjects put up such stubborn resistance? Can't you sell the proposition to them?"

"I had Rickenthorp sold, don't ever doubt it," Drake snarled. Automatically his hand went to his pocket. Of all things, his billfold was safe. At least, that hadn't been a frame-up between Rickenthorp and some henchmen. For the moment Drake felt somewhat relieved.

But as soon as he discovered his gun was missing his suspicions rose, his temperature mounted, and his head, already aching like fury, was suddenly full of blowtorches.

"We are in one devil of a jam, Doc. Somebody's lifted my pistol. There'll be hell busting loose around here before we know it."

The doctor's bleary eyes came down from the ceiling to focus upon Drake. "But what have we done? Nothing except to pursue our rightful scientific interests. My experiments will some day be acclaimed by all the world."

"Yeah? You think you're so damned innocent, don't you?"

The words struck fire in the wizened doctor's watery eyes.

"Of course, I'm innocent. You've told me a hundred times over that everything we're doing is perfectly legal."

"All right, all right." The thick-faced man closed his eyes and ran his fingers through his hair savagely.

"You've told me," the doctor pursued, "that you have taken care of everything. I am a man of science. I have no time to delve into the legal tangles that might hamper us. But you have assured me—"

"Forget it, I said. I don't want to hear any more about it."

But the argument was by no means ended. The next day the doctor began his worried mumblings afresh. He haunted Drake for one assurance after another. In desperation, Drake piled the lies high: of course the proper authorities had been consulted; of course these experiments were licensed; everything would go on as usual.

"Don't pay any attention to what I said last night. I was probably out of my head."

THE doctor countered with a gleam of logic. "If everything is all right, why were you attacked?"

"I told you," Drake hedged, "that was just some damned eves-dropping ignoramus. The public can't appreciate what we're doing. But it won't happen again. From now on we'll keep this place guarded."

There was no use confiding any more to Dr. Silverhead. The less he knew the better. It would be a lucrative game only so long as Drake and his two henchmen kept the whys and wherefores under their hats.

But it was a cinch that something had gone haywire the previous evening. How in the devil had Hamilton Craig managed to show up at that time of evening. The henchmen would have to answer for that.

The more Drake puzzled over this, the more the aching from the previous night's blows blasted his brain. In his racket, careful timing was everything. He had known that Hamilton Craig was in the Overton Employment office late in the afternoon. And afterward that Craig was lined up with a few engagements for the rest of the evening.

Craig was not a man to miss his appointments.

Why, then, had Craig been found on these premises at the very time he was not wanted?

If Drake could have answered that question, he might have had the key to the whole fiasco.

Unfortunately, Craig *had* shown up, and so Drake's two strong-arm men had been forced to take him for a walk. And that had left the approaches to Drake's conference room unguarded.

Drake's strong-arm men were Mac and Krug, and they would have to answer for their activities after leaving with Craig, for it was high noon the following day and they still had not returned.

Drake puffed at the orchid cigarette holder. The empty hallways echoed his impatient pacing.

"When those two lazy louts come in," he told Dr. Silverhead, "send them through to the court. I'm going out and tend my garden."

Drake descended to the basement, donned a pair of coveralls, and sorted over his garden tools. A pleasurable thrill of anxiety surged through him as he made his selection. This was his most useful tool—a pair of pruning shears.

He held them up to the light of the basement window and scrutinized the razor-sharp cutting edge.

As he ascended the steps and wandered out into the enclosed court, he was thinking of a walrus-mustached gentleman named Rickenthorp. If he knew his clients, that gentleman would be too scared to say anything today. A badly frightened man doesn't grow bold overnight.

But by next week Rickenthorp would be telling everyone about his narrow escape.

Or would he?

Drake was smiling inwardly now. He snipped off the top of a hollyhock plant, twisted it in his fingers until he reached the old-fashioned well in the center of the court. He bent over the circular brick wall. With his pruning shears he sliced away at the hollyhock bud. The fragments fell noiselessly into the shaft of bottomless blackness.

Suddenly Drake was startled by a pleasant voice only a few yards away.

"Hello, sir. Interesting garden you've got here."

Drake thrust the pruning shears into his coveralls' pocket. Before him stood a well-dressed young man with quick eyes and a hint of nervousness in his smile.

"What do you want?" asked Marcus M. Drake.

"Just thought I'd drop around and get acquainted with Dr. Silverhead. My name's Archie Burnette."

CHAPTER NINE
Green Lights for Murder

MARCUS M. DRAKE had a natural aversion to strangers, especially those that seemed to have their wits about them. This young fellow was alert. But he was too young and naive to know much, Drake thought.

"We may be able to use you around here," Drake said presently, after he had listened to the young man's recitation about being hired by Craig, the owner of this property. "So Craig told you to drop around and get acquainted with the Doctor, did he? Not a bad idea."

"You work here too?" the young man asked.

"Oh, I putter around in the garden just to pass the time. I'm sorta looking after the doctor. He's got no business judgment whatsoever. The absentminded old duffer would let his rent slide for months if it wasn't for me." Drake decided that the newcomer was swallowing his line.

"Not making much, huh?"

"Well, just between you and me, he's got a damned good thing as soon as it hits. That's why I'm staying with him. But don't worry, I'll see that Craig gets all the rent that's coming to him. I just hope he won't be in a hurry for it."

"I'll urge Mr. Craig to hold off with any possible eviction notices and give your delinquent doctor a chance."

When Drake heard this, his suspicions were eased.

"The doctor's through that door?" asked Archie.

"That's right. You'll find him at work in there. Tell him Drake sent you in to look around. And think nothing of it if he never even sees you. He's that way. And one thing more—don't let him use you in any of his experiments."

"Why not?"

The kid was still wet behind the ears, Drake thought.

"Because we don't let anybody go through the Doc's experimental procedures unless we register him and give him a physical test and all that."

"Sounds good," said the young man as he went on his way.

Drake slapped the pruning shears against his side, satisfied. Things would be easier than ever with this stooge of Craig's on the grounds. Now if only those two lazy louts, Mac and Krug, would get back from the previous night's fiasco, there might be some green lights ahead.

But Drake knew there were still a couple of problems to contend with. His headache was back again in full fury. He stomped along the path, snipping at every straggling branch he passed, thinking intensely. One of those problems was discovering the identity of his anonymous assailant from the previous evening. Who was he? Where had he come from? Was he a friend of Rickenthorp? Apparently he had been content to free the walrus-mustached gentleman and let it go at that. He hadn't even bothered to recover the money, and evidently he hadn't seen fit to call the police.

But he had taken the gun—a black pistol with a corrugated handle that Drake would know anywhere.

It was the work of an amateur, Drake decided—someone who had bumped in on the conference scene accidentally.

Drake's other problem was this man, Craig. He was still an enigma showing up unexpectedly when he was thought to be elsewhere.

Just then Mac Macklevitch and his buddy Krug straggled into the court. Drake was waiting for them with a full head of steam.

WITH careless unconcern Mac rubbed his crooked nose and twisted the tufts of hair that bristled from his scarred right eyebrow. Krug also listened with a show of indifference, all the while whistling little tunes through his teeth. But Drake gave them their orders in no uncertain terms.

"Something slipped last night, and it came near being the end of us. Another break like that and we'll be looking for a new address."

"What happened, boss?"

"Take a look at the stairway up to the conference room. Take a good look, and figure out if you can who slammed me over the skull with a chair. That's your first job, gents. Trace it down and don't miss anything.

"Second, you've got to bump off Rickenthorp. *He missed the mill.* We had him on his way when the lights went out—and I went with 'em.

"Third job is to get an angle on Craig."

"We're not worried about him, boss. He went out and played table tennis with us like a pal. We kept him at it till we figured your deal was over."

"You figured wrong," Drake growled. "And it's not the first time, you know that."

"But, boss," Mac raised his scarred eyebrow cheerfully. "We've sewed him up. He's right in the palm of our hand. And a Craig in the hand is worth two hundred thousand or so in the sock—ain't it so, Krug?"

"Cut out the gags and tell him what we've done," said Krug.

"What *have* you done?" Drake studied the two thugs skeptically. They'd better not start having ideas of their own.

"We've landed jobs with Craig," said Mac, "keepin' watch on this place while he remodels it. He's got a young fella named Burnette on daytime duty, and he's gonna hire a landlady and a staff of girls to run the office end of the mansion—"

"It's an advertising stunt," Krug explained.

"And right away they'll start renting apartments in this building to workers and their families," Mac went on.

"The hell!" Drake growled. "Can't you stall him off?"

"It's easier than that. Ain't we the night watchmen? All right, we guard the place from ten o'clock on. Your customers come right in, same as always, on a one-way ticket."

"Well…it doesn't sound too bad I suppose," said Drake, still feeling a little doubtful.

"It's good," said Krug. "He trusts us."

"It may work for awhile," Drake continued.

"It'll work until the remodeling gets back to our half of the building. What more could you ask?"

Drake gave a low laugh. "By then we'll have lined our pocketbooks with enough cash that we'll be able to retire. If things don't go as well as we hope then we'll hit up Craig for an *extension*. Who knows, he might even find himself so tangled up in Doc Silverhead's web by that time."

With this outlook Marcus M. Drake forgot his headache and went about his gardening.

Before a week passed, the delightful little scheme for swindling and murdering the doctor's prospective investors seemed to be back on a smooth track. The walrus-mustached Mr. Rickenthorp had been quietly bumped off. The newly employed guards were on their job. The doctor's mysterious experiments continued, completely in secret, and the surrounding public—including one Archie Burnette—never guessed that the doctor's vision was to be able to *change one person into two—so that any man could have as many duplicates as he wanted.*

CHAPTER TEN
Verrazzano in Distress

ARCHIE BURNETTE'S visit to the laboratories of Dr. Silverhead left him in great consternation. It was more than he could fathom. What did a successful businessman like Hamilton Craig mean by allowing the doctor to carry on such a mysterious enterprise on these premises?

As Archie wandered back to the oaken reception room, he felt compelled to bring matters to a decision. Either he must walk out on this job or he must ally himself to Hamilton Craig, come what may.

"Darned if I can figure that guy out," Archie said to himself. "He's as jumpy as a grasshopper—always turning up in a new place. I can't figure him out."

Archie was recalling Craig's words of that morning: "Was I drunk? …Never mind."

It would seem that Craig had no recollection of his activities of the previous evening.

Was it possible that this successful young architect was a split personality? In his role as a businessman, could he forget that he was harboring a group of criminals in these buildings? Or was he somehow innocent?

Archie needed the job, but it wasn't that which made his decision take root so much as another factor. In his pocket was the mysterious book containing six cards—no, five— Cornelia was absent. At any rate, it was Archie's natural curiosity regarding this strange phenomenon that helped him decide to stay on.

Heavy footsteps sounded outside the entrance, and the vast form of Carlo Verrazzano, the perfume salesman, appeared. He lifted his hat, made a graceful bow, and looked about eagerly.

"Ah, sir, you are the verree man I weesh to see!"

Archie placed himself back of the desk and prepared to resist a sales talk. The big man was smiling down at him, making grandiose gestures. Archie only stared at him coldly.

"What can I do for you?"

"The *beautiful* Cornelia," he said with a flourish. Alas…she has gone. But I think she come here, maybee?"

"You're barking up the wrong tree, friend. I haven't seen her. What makes you think she would come here?"

"Ah, she have a queeck talk with Mr. Craig. They make business plans. And when she come back to me she only talk money, money, money."

Verrazzano's face grew sad, and he touched his eyes with a handkerchief. "No longer she smile at me so sweet."

"Well, what then? Did she walk out on you?"

"It all happen so sudden I really do not know."

"Where did you leave her…at Craig's office?"

"No, no, no. It was while we were having dinner that Mr. Craig come and talk. When he was gone, she no more listen to my stories, how I sell ten thousand, twenty thousand dollars of the gorgeous perfume. I have her walk with me in the Italian garden. Ah, eet is beautiful. The heaven full of stars—sweet music. Dancing."

"You were at a night club? She got away from you in the garden?"

"She disappears from me like that!" Verrazzano snapped his fingers.

Archie scowled. "I don't like this, Verrazzano. I'm responsible for that girl. I'll have to go and find her."

THE perfume salesman's calf-like eyes brightened with hope. "You weel bring her back to me?"

"Let me get this straight," said Archie. "Stars, music and dancing—and so you tried to kiss her."

"Ah, you were there?"

"And then she disappeared."

"So! You saw eet happen!"

"I saw nothing," said Archie, "but I will go and find her if you will give me the address. Poor girl, she probably was trampled under foot."

"The address, I have eet here. So I would remember, I queeck wrote eet on a card that I find on the floor."

Archie scrutinized the card that the sad-faced Romeo was handing him.

"For safekeeping," said Archie smiling, "I'll pack it away in this little book. Run along, pal, and stop your sniveling. Your Cornelia is safe and sound."

Senor Verrazzano made three deep bows and gushed his appreciation that his Cornelia would not be lost. He offered Archie a taxi ride to the nightclub to effect the rescue and made other suggestions that Archie found equally ridiculous. In the end, Verrazzano had to be satisfied with leaving his telephone number, in hopes that Cornelia would call him.

When the temperamental Italian was gone Archie laughed to himself. Cornelia was again safe in the book.

That evening Craig came to the mansion to set forth some further instructions. As rapidly as these rooms could be made over into apartments, the business of renting them would proceed. And the six girls who made up the pages of Craig's book had indeed landed a contract.

"We will utilize their picture in our newspaper advertisements," said Craig. He laid before Archie a photograph that had been taken during the parade. The six girls, all dressed in colorful Oriental costumes would serve as an attractive eye-catcher in any ad.

"So Cornelia got you to sign on with her and the other the girls?" asked Archie.

"Cornelia—yes. Do you know her? She's a very fine businesswoman. Now if you will excuse me, I have some business calls to make."

As Archie retreated through the copper-studded doorway to the reception room, he pondered the strangeness of Craig's words—did not Craig remember the meeting of the three of them that morning? It was curious that his memory was so hazy.

Now Archie could hear a telephone chat, highly informal, as if between two old friends. And to Archie's astonishment, Craig was reciting the full story of his adventure of the previous evening. This time his memory seemed to be fresh on every detail.

"They were just a pair of pick-up friends that I happened to meet at a bar...Mac Macklevitch and Krug. They're all right. Darned good at table tennis...sure, I'll be seeing more of them. Fact is, I've hired them to help around here...he told you? ...Oh, him...yes, he seems to be pretty reliable."

And then Craig's voice became so low that Archie could no longer hear.

As Archie retired to a third floor room that had been assigned to him, he knew he was too confused over these growing mysteries to formulate any theory toward their solution. The last words he had heard Craig say over the phone to his mysterious friend were: "We had better talk this over together. Can you risk coming out yet tonight? It will be late enough that no one will see you."

As Archie was about to fall asleep, he heard a car stop in front of the mansion. He peered out the window. Coming up the walk was a tall, straight young man that Archie would have sworn in court was none other than Hamilton Craig.

CHAPTER ELEVEN
The Literal Doctor

THERE should have been traffic lights in the reception room to handle the crowds in the days that followed. The mansion suddenly became the busiest place on Southwest Boulevard.

The carpenters and plasterers and decorators were supposed to use a side entrance, but they continually found their way into the front office, as the white tracks on the oak flooring attested.

And prospective renters—they came in droves. Nine-tenths of them came merely out of curiosity. Many were attracted by the clever advertising in the daily papers.

The north wing of the old hospital was being transformed rapidly. A few sample apartments were already being exhibited.

As the advertisements had promised, visitors were conducted through the building by beautiful girls—the "Craigettes."

Archie was amazed to see how this advertising scheme worked. He had supposed that these six girls in his book would rebel at the idea of remaining prisoners, so to speak, of Hamilton Craig. In their readiness to assume their duties as usherettes, they were virtually automatons. That is, they would emerge from hiding whenever they were needed. Archie had only to remove a card from the book, toss it into the air, and count to ten. A beautiful usherette would appear before him.

Craig was unquestionably pleased with the way things were going. But he was by no means complacent. He had an eye out for trouble, and Archie soon realized that he was worried on two counts.

One of these worries had to do with the usherettes, the other with Dr. Silverhead. He would frequently call Archie in for conference.

"Who is the new girl who was on duty this morning?"

"The platinum blonde? Her name's Genevieve."

"Genevieve—oh, yes. I remember choosing her for the parade. Hollywood stuff, that gal. What's she like when you get to talking with her?"

Archie shrugged. "We're not speaking. She can't see me."

"That's strange. Whenever she passes this door she sends me a smile that would do for a toothpaste ad."

"That's because you're Hamilton Craig," said Archie. "Besides, she's practicing for movie close-up, or I miss my guess. When she first materialized she walked straight to a mirror. That's where she's been most of the time since."

Archie then brought his finger to his lips in a gesture for silence as the platinum blonde passed just outside the office door, leading a party of wealthy sightseers. Archie waved, but Genevieve refused to acknowledge him.

"Look at her give me the cold shoulder. There's a snob if I ever saw one." Archie said softly.

Craig smiled and asked, "What happened? Did you two quarrel?"

"I laughed at her," said Archie. "You see when Benjamin Dodge, the electrician, came in to inspect our wiring, Genevieve took him for a prospective tenant. She showed him all around and brought him down and tried to sign him up for an apartment. Then he told her who he was, thanked her and walked out. He took the wind out of her sails. I sat there laughing, and she hasn't been speaking to me since."

Craig nodded, mildly amused. He walked to the office door, and his eyes followed Genevieve out of sight.

Another party arrived. Archie caught his cue. He opened the book, tossed out a card, and presently Hetty was before him, her snappy black eyes facing him accusingly.

"Archie, have you straightened out that matter—?"

"The customers are waiting, Hetty."

"But Archie, I have got to talk with you."

"The customers—Miss Hildreth," Craig cut in.

OBEDIENTLY Hetty went on her way. Craig had been disturbed before by Hetty Hildreth's behavior. She seemed always to have some personal problem for which she demanded Archie's attention.

"It's about a picture she took," Archie started to explain. "I think we ought to talk about it. Once you suggested that we have luncheon together, the three of us."

Craig frowned. "Did I suggest that? Well, I'm much too busy."

There was Craig's memory gone rusty again. All right, let him forget his former interest in Hetty. Archie would not be the loser.

That afternoon Craig had a long conference with Dr. Silverhead. When the office door finally opened and the white-haired doctor shuffled away mumbling to himself, Archie was called in. He found Craig smoking nervously, looking haggard.

"Sit down, Archie." Craig paced from one window to another, rarely facing Archie. "It beats the devil how a man can be as smart as that doctor and still too dumb to talk straight English."

"Can't you get him to pay his rent?" Archie asked. "Or are you trying to move him out?"

Craig crushed his cigarette in the ashtray.

"It goes much deeper than that. What I'm about to tell you is strictly confidential. A slick district attorney could do me plenty of damage if he got wind of this."

Archie waited, choked with silence. Could it be that Craig had let himself in for a share in Silverhead and Drake's shady racket?

"It all started innocently enough," Craig said. "Being a bachelor with money, I found myself subject to all sorts of intrusions—solicitors and agents for charity, social butterflies, and what not. I suppose I should have hired a hard-boiled doorman, who would simply turn people away. But I took a notion to have some fun, and that was the 'fatal step' so to speak."

Craig chuckled lightly as he recalled his first experiments in equipping his house with mechanical ghosts, black cats and hoot owls.

"I wanted a dancing skeleton, and someone referred me to Dr. Silverhead. That's when I got in…maybe a little over my head."

"I don't understand."

"He took me too literally. He came through by bringing in a man who was literally a living skeleton. Where he got the poor fellow, or how he got him, I don't know. It still gives me the creeps when I think of entering my house to discover that gruesome heap of skin and bones dancing to his death in my doorway."

Archie shuddered. "What—what happened?"

"Never mind," said Craig, "that's all past. I resolved not to repeat that mistake. But having located Dr. Silverhead here on Southwest Boulevard, I saw my chance to take over these buildings as a real estate investment. Of course I'd like to eventually to get rid of the doctor."

"Won't he go peaceably?"

Craig shook his head dubiously. His past conferences with the doctor had left him even more uncertain about what to do.

"He leaves all business matters to his 'gardener,' Drake. But I certainly don't want to get mixed up with him. I'd get them both out of here yet today if I could be sure the action wouldn't boomerang on me. But the doctor knows things, he has a chokehold on me. In fact, a couple of them."

"The skeleton in the doorway…"

"The other matter was the 'transformation' of these girls into cards—an incredible feat of science to be sure. Could you ever have imagined anything like this? Silverhead is an eccentric genius almost beyond scientific comprehension. He's discovered things no scientist could scarcely dream of— all here in this deserted medical facility. Yet in many ways he's a total nincompoop, almost unable to function in the everyday world. And now I'm knee deep in his madness. Maybe there aren't any specific laws to cover such unusual cases, but I'd hate to stand trial in the courts for what happened when those girls walked through that copper-studded doorway."

AT LAST Archie knew he was getting next to the source of this strange phenomenon. Was it true that Craig had deliberately conceived this scheme and employed a scientist to carry it out?

"Again I protest my innocence," Hamilton Craig said. "It was that doctor's damnable habit of interpreting orders *literally*. I thought I was giving him a harmless instruction. I said, 'All I want you to do is to fix something in this office doorway to make people go away.' Note my words: 'make people go away.' "

"I get it," said Archie.

"So did the doctor. But I didn't. Even when he wrote my words down on paper and had me sign my name, I didn't guess the incredible thing that was in his mind. I remember that he inquired whether I meant to get rid of them for good. I replied that they could leave their cards—I meant 'business' cards—that would be sufficient. Then he jotted down something more and said I should leave it to him; he would fulfill my orders to the letter."

Archie found himself gazing in awe at the row of copper points in the Gothic doorway. "And so—"

"And so a few weeks later, as I was making ready to move in here, I received a written report from the doctor, informing me that the experiment had been successful. Rats and guinea pigs were *two-dimensionalized,* as he called it, by this new instrument, and he had now installed it in my office doorway. Anyone who entered while the switch was on would immediately undergo a molecular transformation, being reduced in size to a card that would fit neatly into an address book."

"Ye gods!" Archie gasped.

"I received this word—umm—by telephone soon after the parade. I was told that the six girls were already on their way out to see me. When I came in and snapped the switch off, I found here on my desk six cards waiting for me. The deed had been done."

Craig was pacing the floor again. Archie found himself in a mental whirlpool.

"If I understand you correctly, Mr. Craig, you did not intend it to happen this way—in spite of your plan to choose from these six girls for your marriage."

"My marriage?" Craig turned sharply. And there was anger in his surprised query. "Who said anything about marriage?"

Archie drew back defensively. "But you told me yourself that within thirty days you expected to marry one of these—"

"Did I say that? Oh…" For a moment Craig stood speechless, shifting his eyes from Archie to the telephone and to the office door. He regained his poise.

"All right, I seem to have told you everything. Anyway, you can see I'm in a devil of a jam until I get rid of this devilish doctor. No telling what he'll do next. I have tried to put him to work on this problem of bringing the girls back to their normal state *permanently.*"

"Evidently he can do anything," Archie commented sarcastically.

"He wouldn't give me any satisfaction," said Craig. "He said it would take lots of experimenting before he could undo what he has done. And he rambled on with some theories that all living matter may have progressed from a two-dimensional state into a three. He thinks the guinea pigs he transformed have a strong instinct to lapse back into the two-dimensional state whenever they face a crisis."

"Does Marcus M. Drake know about all this?" Archie asked anxiously.

"I doubt it. The doctor is not communicative. But the minute I put him under too much pressure he may confide in Drake. When that happens, they will build a fire under me."

CHAPTER TWELVE
Vision of Murder

WOULD Hamilton Craig marry before his thirty days were up?

As long as Archie kept busy at the mansion he could almost forget the importance of that question. But when he was called downtown for a private conference in the architect's studio, he always came away realizing that this matter outweighed everything else.

"Out of any half dozen good looking girls," Craig had said during one particular visit, "there ought to be at least one that could endure being married to a stubborn bachelor like me."

"The wrong attitude," Archie had commented mentally, but not aloud. *Any one of those girls could go for you in a big way if you'd quit acting like women are poison.*

For Hamilton Craig did act that way, Archie thought. When it came to snobbery, the platinum blonde named Genevieve had nothing on Hamilton Craig. Wasn't it a bit absurd, thought Archie, that in spite of all the time Craig spent in the mansion while these usherettes were coming and going on all sides of him, he should call Archie downtown to discuss these girls, one by one?

"You should know them as well as I do," Archie had said bluntly on one occasion.

"I think I'm best acquainted with Hetty, from what you've told me. But you'd better name them over again. Not too fast, Archie."

"Hetty...Cornelia...Genevieve...Grace...Patsy...and Linda Lee. There you are. Take your choice. They're six of a size, all beautiful, and all probably in love with you."

"Not so fast, Archie. Tell me about them again—slowly. You may skip Hetty. She's the camera girl with the snappy brown eyes—the one who went with you the night you spied on Drake and the doctor. And you may skip Cornelia. I discovered her adoration for me and my checkbook in two minutes. But she has a good business head. The contract she dragged out of me is proving a good investment. Next—— Genevieve."

"Genevieve and I still aren't speaking," said Archie. "I'm not high-toned enough for her. Maybe it's because she's a platinum—or it might be that she has ancestors."

"Yes, I've heard about her."

"Heard about her? She wastes a smile on you every time she passes you."

"Do I—uh—return the courtesy?" This was too much for Archie. If Hamilton Craig was so absent-minded that Genevieve's expensive smiles failed to penetrate, he'd better remain a bachelor, and let the uncle's fortune go to charity.

"To finish calling the roll, there's Grace, Linda Lee, and Patsy. Grace never has much to say except when she's checking up on the rights and wrongs of something. She has such a busy conscience that I feel guilty every time I see her. But she says she'll work as long as you don't profiteer on your tenants or tell any white lies in your sales talks. She's very strict. You can see it in those cold green eyes."

"Yes, very strict but very attractive," observed Craig. "Next—Linda Lee."

"She's the Southern gal that chatters on and on like a meadowlark without a care in the world...and Patsy...she's the red-head that carries chips on each shoulder. She'd rather fight than eat. Nothing's happened so far that hasn't made her mildly furious. She got sore waiting for her pay, but she was a helluva lot sorer when she got it. I figured you'd fire her the first time she angered a customer."

"I suppose I should—"

"But the customers seem to fall for her, in spite of the belligerence. Her record is still tops."

"Remarkable."

"That's exactly what you said when I told you all this yesterday. Look here, Mr. Craig. Is it possible that Dr. Silverhead has done something to you so that you have two sets of memories—one for this downtown studio, and the other for the office out at the mansion?"

Archie meant this question to be taken as facetious, even though it was a joke born of exasperation. But Craig caught his breath, his eyes blinked defensively, and he made no answer. He was blushing.

"Heck, I—I didn't mean anything serious, Mr. Craig," Archie stammered, hastening to cover over this mysterious something he had crashed into. "I know you're a very busy man. I'll be helping you every way I can."

"I'm depending upon you. In fact," Craig concluded in a confidential tone, "I'm going ahead with the arrangements for the wedding."

"And the lucky girl is—?"

"One of the six Craigettes," Craig said with a chuckle. "It's much too early to settle on the final details."

NOW Archie sat in the barroom just off Southwest Boulevard munching a corned-beef sandwich. This slightly dank beer joint was one place where Archie could be alone with his thoughts. A sour-looking stranger with deep circles around his eyes was growing drowsy over a drink. The bartender was lost in his newspaper. The jukebox was thumping away with heavy rhythm and a minimum of melody.

This place would soon be gone, Archie reflected. The little lobby and the dilapidated apartments that filled this west wing of the old hospital building were due for an overhauling, and Craig was the architect with the magic touch.

Archie couldn't see who the two men were who occupied the end booth; much less could he catch any of their low-spoken conversation audible between jukebox records. But he caught sight of a stubby brown hand tapping a monocle on the tabletop. It was a gesture that sent chills racing through Archie's spine.

"Change, please," Archie said, abruptly, forgetting to finish his sandwich.

He walked down to the end of the block, crossed the street, loafed along the windows, all the while keeping a sharp eye on the beer joint.

No one came or went.

"I'm in no hurry," Archie said to himself. "I'll stick around."

He killed half an hour walking up and down the street and finally sauntered into a lonesome hamburger den. Here he had a good view across the street and down most of the block.

"Two hamburgers and two coffees, pal," he said. "My friend will be here shortly."

While the man had his back turned frying hamburgers, Archie got out his little leather book and chose a card with care. He flipped it into the air.

"I've ordered for you, Hetty." Archie had opened and closed the outside door so the hamburger man wouldn't be too surprised over the new arrival. A girl as pretty as Hetty, dressed in a bright Oriental costume—the official uniform of the Craigettes—was sure to make any man look twice.

"Pray, what are we doing here?" Hetty asked in a guarded tone.

"Keeping our eyes open for trouble," Archie whispered. "Gosh, you look as fresh as a daisy. What do you dream when you're packed away in my notebook?"

"Dream? I've forgotten what the word means," said Hetty. "It's the blankest sensation you can imagine—like some sort of long-lost rest that you've been craving all your life."

"You'll have to tell me more when there's time. For Craig's sake we've got to find out how to get you girls over these magic transformation processes. But we'll talk about that later. Just now..." Archie made certain that only Hetty could hear him, "…it's that tavern door…I'm sure Marcus M. Drake is putting the screws on a new prospect."

Hetty's sharp brown eyes were full of questioning.

"Archie, I've missed out on almost everything since that one dreadful night. Did you and Mr. Craig ever get the police on the job?"

"No. Not exactly. But Craig says the police know about Dr. Silverhead. They think he's eccentric but harmless."

"Archie, in this camera I have a photograph that would *convict*—" Hetty broke off sharply, for the hamburger man had been distracted from his radio. She resumed her whispering. "Why, Archie? *Why* hasn't Craig set the law on those boys? Well?"

"I can't answer that, Hetty."

THE girl's eyes grew hot with suspicion. "Archie, I don't want to be jumping at conclusions. But it looks to me as if our boss is mixed up in a murder racket."

"No—you're mistaken."

"Then tell me why he doesn't get busy and clean it out, Archie." She was clutching his hand, searching his eyes intently. "Please, Archie, if you have an answer, tell me. I couldn't bear to think that you might be in on it too."

Archie's heart beat fast. Her words somehow took his breath away—as if it mattered so much to her that he kept clear of trouble. Suddenly he was feeling the burden of this trouble as never before. This trap was closing in, slowly but surely, and his good friend Hamilton Craig was caught in it.

"Maybe it isn't what we think," Archie suggested, making a foolish attempt to be optimistic. "Maybe the doctor's experiments would be no more serious than—say, for example—transforming people so they can be carried as cards in a book."

"I suppose you consider *that* an honorable experiment."

"Well, to tell the truth," said Archie, "I'm a little surprised that there hasn't been any real complaint on the part of you girls. In fact you seem to be enjoying yourselves."

"We *seem* to be—for two or three good reasons," said Hetty, a note of bitterness in her tone. "Some of us girls are dead certain there'll be a pot of gold at the foot of this rainbow for one of us, if we can hold on until Hamilton Craig makes his choice. For my part that's so much foolishness. But if I were going to drag someone like you or Dr. Silverhead or Hamilton Craig into the criminal courts for involving me in a magic trick that keeps me out of social circulation half the time, do you think I'd go around fore-warning you? No. So there may be a second reason that we girls *seem* to be complacent. Think it over and weep."

"I'll just think it over," said Archie. "Any more reasons?"

"The third one is real, no question about it. There is a satisfaction—a peace beyond that of any sleep—that comes whenever we transform into our inanimate selves." Hetty drew a deep breath. "The wonder is that we're so willing to come back to normal life whenever you call us."

Archie attended these words as if they were messages from another world—a glimpse of some weird realm of life that he would never know.

As a result of these ponderings he felt an unexpected throb of admiration and respect for the strange scientific accomplishments of recent days. Then he looked across the street to see Dr. Silverhead trudging along. It was an emotion he hadn't intended, being utterly opposed to the judgments that were guiding the doctor's actions. But the feelings were there, nevertheless, and it was an honest admission that yonder crack-brained scientist must have seen his way into some remarkable miracles.

"Do I see Drake and his guest at the tavern doorway?" Hetty asked.

Across the street the three men had assembled—Drake, Dr. Silverhead, and their tall, well dressed "guest." Evidently Drake was introducing this newcomer to the doctor, for there was a moment of handshaking. Then the doctor hurried on his way.

In another minute the conference ended, Drake disappeared into the tavern, and the tall stranger strode down the street.

Archie wanted to follow him, but he thought better of it. Undoubtedly, Drake's eyes were following this man to make sure there were no officers on the trail. Archie turned to Hetty.

"Would you know him if you saw him again?"

"I think so," said Hetty. "Notice how he carries his left shoulder higher than his right, and keeps looking around as if he thought someone was watching him."

"We're lucky if someone isn't watching us," said Archie. "We had better have another coffee."

Hetty was looking at him curiously. "I know what you're planning, Archie. You're going to keep guard over that conference room again tonight. Aren't you? ...Well, I'm going with you. This is my deal as much as yours."

Archie caught her by the arm and started to draw her toward him.

"No," said Hetty, drawing away from him. "Don't you dare put me back in the book!"

ARCHIE'S and Hetty's watch for the return of the "high-shouldered stranger" extended through the next three days and nights. The man did not return, and they decided he must have rejected Marcus M. Drake's investment plan. They relaxed their vigilance.

Nevertheless, Archie was on the alert. His habits of watching and listening for signs of danger could not be turned off like electric lights. In his room he had placed his bed near the west window, where he could keep watch over the court, and there he was sleeping on the night of his terrifying dream.

From the strenuous three days past, Archie was dog-tired, and on this night he meant to get a solid night's sleep. His last comforting thought was that no lights burned in Drake's conference room.

Soon he was lost in sleep, and then came the dreadful series of nightmares. Weird and fantastic images played through his mind, trying to startle him out of his rest. But through it all he kept resolving not to be disturbed. These phantasmagoric pictures, these shifting shadows, these creeping creatures of the night were but the stuff of dreams.

Nevertheless, one of these scenes cut such a deep path through his troubled mind that he seemed to see it over and over through the rest of the night. At dawn he awoke and stared dizzily into the courtyard. That was where it had happened in his dream, a moonlight murder that had haunted him all night long.

He looked down. There were the steps he had seen in his dream, the circling path, the extending arms of hollyhocks that had brushed them as they passed—those two shadowy figures who had walked to the well.

In the scene before Archie's eyes, every detail was perfect. He knew the very spot where the two men had stood in his dream as they looked over the low wall into the well. The man on one side had been Marcus M. Drake. The other was the tall, high-shouldered stranger. The quick flash of scissors blades had come from Drake's right hand. From the tall stranger had come the stifled outcry mingled with choking and gurgling.

At that instant, the steel-bladed tool had been tossed aside, and Drake's arms had hurled the other man headlong into the black well. In Archie's nightmares the rest had been a series of sounds—the heavy splash that echoed up from the depths, the long stillness, then the slow tread of Drake winding his way back to the arcade. And later, the thin spray of water that played over the walls and the stone railing and the well.

If Archie had been sure this was only a nightmare, he would have told Hetty all about it. But as the details kept coming back to him clearer and clearer, he decided he must keep this dream to himself.

CHAPTER THIRTEEN
Enter Whiskey Phil

THE leather-upholstered chairs that lined the walls of the oaken reception room were the public's first sample of the comforts and luxuries of Craig's Southwest Boulevard Apartments.

In Archie's opinion, those chairs were much too comfortable. They made the room as inviting as a hotel lobby, and many persons with little or no business would be content to while away a couple of hours on the pretext of waiting to see someone. All of which added to the day's confusion.

This morning Verrazzano was on hand again, inquiring specifically for Cornelia, and angling for an introduction to Genevieve. While he waited he tried to corner a prospective tenant for a perfume sales talk, and Archie had to speak to him.

The sad-eyed man with the concentric circles around his eyes was here again, asking about Grace. As usual he was in a near-stupor from intoxication. Archie had seen him several times at the bar on the west side of the block and by this time knew him to be Philip Parker, better known as Whiskey Phil.

He was an uncle of Grace, the usherette who lived in a realm of such carefully strained morality that she could scarcely breathe without consulting her conscience. He had come several days before to take her home.

But Grace seldom came on duty before noon, and by that time Whiskey Phil was usually too far-gone to remember his mission. He whiled away his cynical forenoons and soggy afternoons in Craig's block, running up a large bill and accomplishing nothing.

This morning Grace was called on duty early, owing to the unaccountable absence of Patsy. As a result, she and her uncle clashed for a showdown.

"You ran out on your home, your family," Whiskey Phil growled. "I'm supposed to bring you back. Not that I give a damn personally."

"I've made my decision," Grace declared. "I won't endure that low environment any longer."

"So it's low, is it? So that's what you think of your home."

"It's low because you're always there, you and the demon that lives in your heart. That's why I was glad to come away."

"But I'm not there, I'm here," Whiskey Phil mocked. "How can you stand it sticking 'round this dump with demons like me around?"

Archie tried to intercede. "In the interests of propriety, Mr. Parker, you should simply state your business and go on your way."

"That's what I'm doing, ain't it? Say, where'd I see you before?"

"I work here for Hamilton Craig," said Archie.

"That's nothing to be so swelled up about. What kind of a joint does Craig run here? Do *you* know? Maybe you do and maybe you don't. If you'd keep your ears open the way I do—ugh, now I know. It was around at the tavern one afternoon. That's where I saw you. You was spying on Drake and that other guy."

Grace tried to apologize for her uncle's blustering. "Please, Uncle, go on your way."

"I'll go when I've found out something—not before. When I go back and your folks ask me all about you, what am I gonna say? How am I gonna convince 'em it took me all these days to get in a word edgewise?"

"Simply tell them the truth," said Grace coldly. "I was always busy and you were always intoxicated."

"But when I came here yesterday, and the morning before, and the day before that, asking for you, why didn't they call you? Where were you?"

THE question brought a deep blush to Grace's cheeks. Her standards of right and wrong wouldn't let her swerve from complete honesty, but this question was hard to answer. Her uncle followed through doggedly.

"If you're in your room, why don't they call you down to see me? Why do they always say they'll have to locate some guy by the name of Archie Burnette—"

"That's me," Archie spoke up, trying to rise to the girl's defense.

"And I suppose," said Whiskey Phil cynically, "you're the housemother of the girls' dormitory, Mr. Burnette?"

"Uncle, you don't understand!" Grace cried, growing as red as fire.

"You're darned right I don't," said Whiskey Phil, pushing toward the door of Hamilton Craig's private office. "But I'm going to. I'll see your boss."

"I can assure you," said Archie, stepping in his path, "that Mr. Craig has hired a matron to supervise the living quarters of these usherettes, if that's what's bothering you. Under ordinary conditions we expect the girls to live in their rooms."

"Yeah? There must be a lot of extraordinary conditions around here, all the trouble they've had trying to find Grace—"

Archie shot out with a good right fist that struck with a heavy smack on the fellow's jaw. The bleary eyes rolled and the puffy rings around them shuddered, but Whiskey Phil didn't go down. He was almost too soggy to feel the blow. It would have taken a freight engine to knock him out.

Nevertheless, he was quite aware that he had been hit, and he changed his mind about walking into Hamilton Craig's office. He stood there gazing at Archie, gazing—strangely enough—in a respectable way. As he spoke he grinned somewhat sheepishly. He rubbed his jaw and spoke.

"I guess that throws a different light on the matter. Don't ask me to explain it, but I think that everything around here is probably on the up-and-up. And anybody knows there never was a straighter gal than—hey! Where is she?"

Archie glanced around the reception room. Verrazzano had cornered two more visitors with his perfume case, and none of them saw what happened to the usherette in the center of the room. The last of the steamy image faded into the air.

Poor Grace! The insults she had picked out of her uncle's careless talk had been too much for her, Archie realized. By this time he knew the secret of these mysterious metamorphoses. Any overwhelming crises were what caused these girls to revert to cards.

Whiskey Phil stood as motionless as a lightning-struck tree for a full thirty seconds. Then he caught Archie by the arm to feel his muscle.

"Talk about a wallop... You don't know your strength, pal. For a minute you had me seeing blind spots.

He looked around as if wondering which exit his niece had taken, not realizing that Archie was packing her away in a leather booklet.

"Tell her to look out for herself," said Whiskey Phil, groping down the steps outside the door. "And she needn't worry about me. I'll be all right as soon as I find a bar."

PATSY, the red-haired usherette with special talents for scrapping, was not among those present on this particular morning.

Her absence was inexplicable. The matron and some of the other girls remembered that she was last seen talking with Hamilton Craig late the previous evening. But no one had heard her speak of leaving for the night.

Now it was mid-forenoon and Craig's office door had not yet opened. Archie knocked. There was no response, so he turned a key and walked in.

Hamilton Craig had evidently left early for his downtown studio. If so, he had neglected to leave a list of instructions on his desk. As a rule, he would call Archie in and deliver the day's orders in person.

Archie's senses were on the alert. The too, too realistic dream of last night's murder by moonlight filled his black mood. He had meant to put some point-blank questions to Craig before any such trifles as rent bills or carpenters' jobs could intrude.

Beyond Craig's office were his living and sleeping rooms and his private entrance on the north side. Archie ventured into the rooms, after receiving no answer to his knock.

Craig's bed had not been slept in.

Archie returned to the private office, picked up the telephone, and called the architect's studio.

Hamilton Craig answered. Archie gave a gasp of relief.

"Anything wrong, Archie?"

"If *you're* all right, there's nothing wrong," said Archie. "I missed seeing you this morning, and when I looked through your rooms just now I decided you must have been out all night."

"Oh, well, that's nothing," Craig laughed. "It could happen to anyone."

"Not that it's any of my business," said Archie, "but do you have one of the usherettes with you?"

"Er—am I supposed to have?"

"Well, the matron and I have accounted for only five this morning, and they say you were talking with Patsy last night—she's the missing one."

Craig laughed, not too comfortably. "Kinda putting me on the spot, aren't you?"

Archie wasn't at all satisfied with Craig's evasive answer. "All right, I'll assume you haven't seen Patsy since last night. I'll send out a search party."

"Better do that. If she's herself, there's no reason to be worried. But if she's changed back to a card, anything could happen. You can't watch those cards too closely."

Archie wanted to know whether Craig would come out early that evening, and as strongly as he dared over the telephone, he suggested that the air was full of trouble. But Craig's responses were exasperatingly indefinite and vague. Archie hung up and walked out.

He walked into the court.

THE fragrance of shrubbery and the bright faces of hollyhocks did nothing to lift his mood. The beauty of these surroundings was to him the camouflage of a trap. He was moving through the territory of his enemy.

He forced himself to walk leisurely, to seem unconcerned. But the arcade of the old hospital building formed an almost complete rectangular enclosure around him. In this moment he could understand the terrors of the claustrophobe.

At the other end of the curved path was Marcus Drake. Archie pretended not to see him, but the snip, snip, snip of the pruning shears could be heard anywhere within the court. A first-rate actor, that man Drake. As he pruned along one might easily believe his whole heart was in this garden.

Archie drew a long, tense breath as he slowly circled the well. His eyes missed nothing. The stone railing had been showered by the garden hose in recent hours. Thin, muddy streams could be seen at the concrete base.

On Archie's third time around the well, he discovered a slight break in the surface of the ground a few feet beyond the base. In his dream, a steel tool had been tossed to the ground. But no longer was that gruesome event a dream. He was coming to grips with reality at last.

Presently he saw Marcus Drake trudging toward him. He pretended not to see. He was interested in looking down the well, as any curious visitor might be.

"Don't fall in there, boy." Drake started to walk on past. Then he turned back. "If you see your boss any time soon, tell him I'd fix this place up if he'd allow me my expenses. Nothing I like better than puttering around in a garden."

"I'll mention it to him," said Archie.

"Maybe you'd like to see the plan I've made."

"Not now, thanks."

Archie peered down at the black water some forty feet below. When he looked up, Marcus Drake was beside him. "Look," said Drake, "those straggling bushes are dying out. We ought to cull them out and plant new ones. I can't stand the sight of anything dead."

"I'll mention it to Craig," Archie repeated. He tried to walk away, but the bogus gardener followed along beside him.

"There should be a few catalpas sprinkled around, too. I've got a symmetrical arrangement worked out." Drake caught Archie's arm and started to lead him off to the right. "It will just take a minute or two to look at this plan."

"No, thanks. I'm busy."

"Hell, you can't be that busy."

Archie glanced at his watch. "I've got an appointment."

"What time?"

"Eleven. I'm five minutes late."

"Important people are always ten minutes late for appointments." Drake tightened his grip on Archie's arm. "The chart is just inside that door."

"Well—"

At that moment someone called to Archie from the office. He was wanted on the telephone. He broke away from Drake's hold and almost ran across the court.

To his surprise the call was not from Hamilton Craig. It was the low, drowsy voice of Philip Parker—Whiskey Phil. Now what could *he* want?

"I been thinkin' Burnette..." Whiskey Phil was considerably more intoxicated than when he had left an hour before, "...you're a good guy, Archie Burnette. Why don't you come around to the tavern and have a drink on me? Maybe I got somethin' interesting to tell you."

CHAPTER FOURTEEN
Craig's Double Personality

BY THE time Archie reached the tavern it was too late.

"He's gone now," said Whiskey Phil. "There was a guy in here you should have seen. He and Mac and that other bum, what's his name—yeah, Krug—they was swappin' lies. And this guy was darn good."

Archie couldn't make anything out of this talk. He should have known better than to let this drunken sot lead him away from his work. And still there was something wise in Whiskey Phil's manner. He was making grotesque faces as he talked, drawing his circled eyes in an exaggerated wink.

"How was this stranger so good?" Archie asked.

"He was a great storyteller, my boy. He kept Mac and Krug in stitches for half an hour."

"Is there anything remarkable about that?"

"Awful funny to watch. Just like the snake I saw at the Zoo. Ever see that snake coil up and blow his neck and spring? That's the way this guy would tell a story. His neck would keep blowing all through the buildup. Then all of a sudden—*snap*—he come out with the point. He had those boys rolling on the floor."

Archie shrugged. He guessed he had better get back to work. But Whiskey Phil tapped him on the wrist.

"This guy—oh, come back some time and you'll get to see him. All right, run out on me. You can't 'preciate a nice dirty place like this. You and Craig have got to go tearing up all this low-down block makin' it over for respectable people. That's a devil of a thing to do. Next thing you know you'll be lighting that inner court up with spots and invitin' the public in for softball or somethin'."

"What gave you that idea?"

"Well, if you do, here's the man that'll fix you up with flood lights."

Whiskey Phil began to scribble on a piece of paper. "His name's Ben Dodge. Now how the hell do you spell it?"

"I think you've got something there, Parker." Archie placed a hand on the drunken man's shoulder.

Archie walked back to the office thoughtfully. Benjamin Dodge was the electrician who had inspected the wiring a few days earlier. It was odd that this dissipated man at the bar should know about him. But apparently he knew a great deal.

Flood lights over the court—that would be the very trick to put an end to these bad dreams.

"Now, why didn't I think of that?" Archie said to himself.

Entering Craig's private office, he called the downtown studio.

"Hello, Mr. Craig. I've got to see you right away—huh?"

"This isn't Craig," came the sharp-edged voice. "He's out. Any message?"

Archie hesitated. He would have sworn that the first "hello" was Craig's enunciation. But this raw twang was not familiar.

"This is Archie Burnette at the Southwest Boulevard Apartments. I'm going to spend some of Mr. Craig's money and I wanted to let him know about it. When will he be back?"

"Couldn't say. When he left he spoke of taking the day off. Do me a favor, will you?"

"What is it?"

"He's had a few business calls here at his studio," said the voice. "If he should drop in out there, have him phone me at once; will you?"

Archie promised and hung up.

Without further ado he took action on Whiskey Phil's ingenious suggestion. He called Benjamin Dodge and ordered a battery of floodlights for the court.

The lights would be expensive and Hamilton Craig might not approve. "He can't do any worse than fire me," Archie said to himself. "And he can't any more fire me than he can evict Dr. Silverhead. I'm too near the inside track—I know too much."

HIS next thought was to urge the tenants to make use of the lighted court in every way possible. Lawn chairs, a drinking fountain, card tables—perhaps even a croquet ground—such improvements would lift this ground right out of the enemy's hands, and there could be no more of those ugly dreams.

But Archie was destined to crash into the immovable Marcus M. Drake long before any of these various improvements could be effected.

"You're scheming something," Hetty said to Archie, lunching with him that noon. "I wish you'd keep me posted on what's happening. I do want to trust you, Archie."

"You've got to trust me, Hetty. I'm plunging on my own now. Things are happening too fast for me to wait on Craig. Besides he's always in a fog."

"What do you mean by that?"

"If I talk with him here he never remembers what he last told me at the studio. If I talk with him down there I have to repeat to him what he's said here before he can get his bearings and talk with me."

"That's strange. He *must* be a good business man."

"I can't figure him out."

Hetty looked up suddenly. "I just thought of something. I'll bet Craig is a sick man."

"Sick? Not that I know of. Why?"

"Otherwise why would he let this awful Dr. Silverhead and Drake stay on? He must be depending on the doctor for something."

"There might be something in that," Archie mumbled. Indeed, there was something. Hetty was hitting closer to the truth than she guessed. But the doctor's invisible chokehold on Hamilton Craig was not to be confided.

"Tell me," said Hetty, as her imagination raced along with this new hypothesis, "is Craig the same when he's downtown?

Are there any differences in his personality, his pep, his habits or anything?"

"Come to think of it," said Archie cautiously, "he is a little different. He always seems more nervous here—chain-smoking and pacing the floor."

"Doesn't he pace the floor of his studio?"

"Not that I recall. He's usually very calm. He doesn't smoke. He's generally thumbing through the stub of a checkbook."

"We're on the right track, Archie," Hetty exclaimed jubilantly, and he had to make a face at her to remind her their talk was confidential. She went on in an intense whisper. "Here's this whole case in a nutshell. Every morning on the way to work he takes the doctor's medicine—vitamins or something—"

"How do you know?"

"I'm just guessing. But look, that makes him full of vim and vigor and business poise and everything, and all the troubles around here are trifling—"

"I wish I could believe that," Archie groaned.

"And he forgets them. But by evening the effect of the medicine has worn off and he lapses into his sick, worried self again—"

"And takes his troubles seriously. Your theory is very pretty, Hetty. But I'd a darn sight rather talk business with him here than down at the studio. If he's sick, I wish he'd stay sick long enough to do some house cleaning around here."

"I wish I didn't keep changing back into a card," said Hetty wistfully. "I'd do some more spying. I'd find out how often he sees Dr. Silverhead. That may be where the men were taking him last night."

"What men?"

"The same two that led him away the first night I was here—you know, the night watchmen—Mac and Krug. I just happened to see the three of them pass the foot of the stairs last night."

Archie got up from the table abruptly. He made a swift circuit of the reception room and Craig's private office and returned to the dining room to Hetty.

"Nobody's located Craig yet," said Archie. "And until we find him we don't have a hint as to where that hot tempered red-head has gone."

"Patsy? Is *she* gone?"

"Hasn't been around since last night. She was last seen talking with Craig. When the two men led him out you didn't see her did you, Hetty?"

The girl shook her head. "N—no. That is—wait a minute. It does seem to me that I saw Craig sticking a white card in his coat pocket..."

CHAPTER FIFTEEN
Three in a Tunnel

THE tunnel was as black as death. Archie groped along on his hands and knees. Again he snapped the flashlight on for a quick glimpse of the dusty walls and ceiling.

It was amazing that there were no tracks through this underground passage.

Now he proceeded through the pitch-blackness, taking care not to brush against the walls. But when he coughed from the dust he felt certain that no one heard him. This trail evidently led away from the haunts of Marcus Drake and the doctor. The entrance from the basement storeroom had been well concealed.

Perhaps this underground passage had been a hiding place during some war in the past. Archie had not come upon it quite by accident. He had been searching for the past three hours for Hamilton Craig. The absence of tracks convinced him that he had lost the trail.

Could he be sure that Hamilton Craig *was* a prisoner of Drake and his henchmen?

That hint had come to him a little earlier through Whiskey Phil. Archie marveled at how much he had gambled on the hunches of this drunken man. The suggestion of Craig's captivity had come shortly after lunch. This time Whiskey Phil had been seen staggering along the curb in front of the mansion, and one of the usherettes had suggested he should be given the bum's rush down the street. Archie had gone after him. As he suspected, Whiskey Phil had some news.

" 'Snone of my bizhness," said Whiskey Phil, sitting down on the curb, "but looks to me like they're bein' 'stravagant, fixin' up so much food on that tray. Must be they've got'n awful important prizner to feed."

Whiskey Phil had grumbled on in this vein. He thought the prisoner might be a king or a senator. "Or it could be some big-shot architect," he had said.

"There's someone else missing," Archie had confided. "One of the usherettes has been gone since last night. Maybe that tray of food—"

"Prob'ly some big-shot architect," Whiskey Phil repeated. Then, as if he had done his good turn for the day, he gave Archie a farewell wave, tipped his hat to the lamppost, and staggered away.

On the strength of that suggestion, Archie had spent the afternoon rambling through the central rooms of the old hospital. He had taken pains not to disturb Drake and the two henchmen in their afternoon council. As long as he had dared, he had listened in, undiscovered. They were plotting for their next victim.

His eavesdropping experience had provided some revelations to Archie. He had learned about the conflict that was heating up between Drake and the two thugs. Mac and Krug were ready to move out. They were sure things were getting much too hot for their health. But the egotistical Drake was so much intoxicated by his own cleverness that he thought they should all stay on.

Drake's argument was that Dr. Silverhead—with all his eccentricities and his mask of genius—was the perfect shield.

"All we have to do is to keep playing cat and mouse with Craig," Drake had insisted. "Tease him along, make him think that some million dollar investments are just around the corner. He'll keep on playing ball if we do."

"It's getting too crowded around here for me," said Mac Macklevitch.

"Those are my sentiments, too" said Krug. "If a racket's good on Southwest Boulevard, it's good at the other end of town, too."

"I make a motion that we start packing," said Macklevitch.

"When we move out," said Marcus Drake, "we won't bother to pack. The doc will never get fixed up in another nest like this for a long, long time—if ever. That's why we've got to stay here for as long as possible. All we'll have to pack is a half a ton of greenbacks when the game runs out. And we'll leave Doc Silverhead hanging to the goal post."

Mac and Krug had hinted that they could do with a few pounds of greenbacks most any time. They were both feeling the need for a vacation in Florida.

AS HE groped along the tunnel, Archie remembered how Drake had silenced them with a gruff bark and reminded them both there was a lot of business on their dockets. At this point Archie had gotten a keyhole glimpse of a sobering demonstration by Drake with his pruning shears.

"One clean snip right over the Adam's apple." Drake had moved toward Mac to make his demonstration more realistic. Mac's eyes lowered to watch the pruning shears flash within a few inches of his throat, and he gave a sickly grin. Drake sat back in his chair, pocketed the shears, and lighted a cigarette. "It's a fine art, boys. Maybe you don't realize you're associating with a top-notch artist."

Krug shrugged uncomfortably. "We don't doubt your ability. But I'd just as soon see this guy Whitmore get his in the doctor's mill. He's stout and wiry, and he's got a neck like a bull calf."

Drake snorted with contempt. "Are you guys yellow? Maybe he hypnotized you with his funny stories."

Then the men had proceeded to talk about their prisoner. In an effort to catch their voices, Archie made the mistake of touching his forehead to the doorknob. The click was followed by a tense silence. Archie slipped away as softly as he could and was out of sight before the door opened. From then on he had explored the doctor's laboratories. Somewhere there must be clues to the hiding place of the prisoner.

The doctor had had a few interruptions in the course of the afternoon. When it was Drake who passed, or Mac or Krug, the scientist had gone on with his monologue uninterrupted.

But once when the pretty Southern usherette, Linda Lee, came that way on an errand, much to Archie's surprise the doctor paused to explain his work. He was busy grinding lenses. His scientific explanations evidently fascinated her.

This was not the first time that Archie had noted a curious attraction between these two. Perhaps Dr. Silverhead's appearance reminded Linda Lee of a venerable Southern colonel. Perhaps she was flattered by his words—words she could not possibly understand. At any rate, this was a rare quirk of the doctor's, that he should come down out of his mystic realm of science to take notice of a human being.

"Mah! It must be wondahful knowing all about these big machines," Linda Lee had said. "Sometime y'all must show me how they work."

If Dr. Silverhead knew anything about any prisoners concealed within this building, he did not mention it. He talked of nothing but lenses.

Down in one of the basement rooms Archie had found a few tracks in the dust of the planks that formed a walk around the heaps of old boxes. He dared to call out in a cautious whisper, "Is anyone here? Is anyone here?"

It was when the voices and footsteps of Mac and Krug had descended upon him that Archie slipped into a remote storeroom. His flashlight had shown him the way back, further and further. Presently he lost the voices, but he discovered a ladder leading down into a pit in a dark corner of this room. He kept calling in a low voice, descending the ladder into the inky darkness. Not the faintest sound encouraged him to follow this trail, nor did his flashlight reveal any signs that this rickety old ladder had been used in recent days. It was only that the pit seemed like a logical hiding place.

The last few feet of descending depended upon a ten-foot rope, tied to the bottom rung of the ladder. Archie searched the bottom of the pit with his flashlight. It looked to be solid earth. But he took no chances. He searched his pockets for something to drop.

A gun, a book of cards, a pocketknife—they were not possessions that he cared to drop in case that dirt floor should prove to be a surface of mud or artificial quicksand.

HE FASTENED the glowing flashlight to his pocket, pointing downward. Then he cautiously climbed down the rope. The light swung about, to reveal a turn of the trail, into a black tunnel leading off from the bottom of the pit.

This gave him more evidence the surface beneath him was probably solid. Nevertheless, when he had reached the knot at the lower end of the rope he hung there trying to touch his toes to the dirt floor beneath him.

Would it be safe to drop?

His question was at once answered.

From high overhead came the groaning and crackling of wood. The hanging ladder suddenly gave way and came down, rope, Archie and all.

For a long moment the hollow pit had resounded with the crashing of rotten timbers. Archie was quick enough with his flashlight to dodge the splintered section of ladder that came flying down like parallel spears. He rolled into the mouth of the tunnel for safety and hovered there until all was silent.

He had thrown his light upward through the pit. He was in one devil of a jam now, he thought. The long ladder had broken under its own weight. The longest remaining section extended about two-thirds of the way up to the surface.

It had seemed a good time to Archie to divest himself of some profanity. He stomped around, cursing his stupidity and calling himself unflattering names. He had had no business coming down here. There had not been one single clue to make him suspect Marcus Drake's prisoner would be hidden here. It was the mystery of an unexplored passage that had led Archie Burnette into this trap. The mystery still eluded him. He could think of no use for such a place as this. But perhaps the tunnel held the answer. On hands and knees he crawled into the low, narrow passage. There was no way to guess how many scores of years ago this tunnel may have been dug. Obviously, it had not been used recently. Archie noted that the air was not stale or dank, as he might have expected in a dead end passage. In fact, there was a draft of air circulating through. Dust from the furnace room had found its way down here. The spade marks in the clay walls were filled.

So here he was then, groping his way through a blackened tunnel. The tunnel kept circling, and Archie soon lost all sense of direction, not to mention distance.

Soon he was in a state of indecision. Was there any reason that he should go on? Perhaps the tunnel extended for miles, though this seemed unlikely, considering the freshness of the air.

Eventually he came to a passage so narrow that he could barely squeeze through on his hands and knees. His clothing seemed much too bulky. He was tempted to store his pocket things in his coat and leave them behind. But presently he made it through this narrows and had smooth sailing again.

He glanced at his watch. Perhaps he could gauge the length of this tunnel by the time required to traverse it. The watch said 6:15—it was earlier than he thought. No matter if he missed dinner; but he must be there to go back and see Craig by eight.

A little farther on he came to the tunnel's end. Abruptly it opened into another pit. His flashlight revealed a curved brick wall. It proved to be a cylindrical shaft about six feet in diameter.

It was the garden well.

TEN feet below the opening of the tunnel, into this brick-walled shaft was the surface of the water. Slowly. Archie combed the walls with an upward spiral of the beam of light. About thirty feet above him was the stone railing, enclosing a patch of dark blue sky.

In Archie's excitement over his discovery, he overlooked the discrepancy between the darkened sky and the time indicated by his watch. At once his curiosity was bounding outward in all directions.

Why should there be a tunnel leading into this well? Could it be a crude means of piping water into the other pit?

What awful mysteries lay buried beneath the surface of that black water? Could Archie explore those mysteries?

Why had this tunnel opening not been visible from overhead?

The latter question was easily answered. The flash beam revealed a projecting ring of brick just above the mouth of the tunnel. That narrow ring must have been just sufficient to cut off the view from above.

A scheme was going through Archie's brain. Perhaps he would not get back to the office by eight. But Opportunity was knocking. He had better answer.

During the next hour he made the long trip back through the tunnel to the other pit. He returned with the rope and a hook, which he had contrived to make out of a piece of wire with which the ladder had once been repaired.

With this crude equipment Archie went fishing in the well. He was working without his flashlight now. He needed to save what little battery there was left. He had reduced the searching process to a set of routine motions. He could hear the hook strike the water. A double arm's length of rope would let it down to the bottom. Then his arm would describe a wide circle and mark across it with slow crisscrossing motions.

The hook caught nothing. Archie could not understand it. Had that moonlight murder been only a dream after all?

Archie had not exhausted his resources. Now he considered a new course of action. If he could fasten the end of the rope securely, he might let himself down, dive into the water and make a thorough search.

Suddenly he was interrupted by the sound of a low, plaintive voice echoing through the tunnel. It was a girl's voice, a childish whimpering.

Archie groped with the flashlight, turning the sickly yellow beam back into the tunnel.

"Who is it? What are you doing down here?" His words melted together as they echoed through the passage. The girl's cry…Archie recognized the voice of Grace. A moment later he found her. She was staring at the flashlight in utter terror. Archie turned the beam on himself.

"Don't be afraid. There's nothing to cry about. You're not hurt, are you?"

For a few moments the girl refused to talk. Archie found it difficult to soothe her. He kept repeating the same statements over and over. "Book lost out of my pocket. But don't worry, I'll get you out of here in a few minutes."

When Grace began to get a grip on herself, her morality complex was quick to come to the fore. How could she ever explain a situation like this? What would people say if they knew that Archie had brought her down to this hidden passage?

Archie almost lost his temper. "Act your age. Is it my fault you came awake at a time like this?"

Then, as he picked up the address book, he was much relieved to find another card in it. He tossed the card into the air.

"Maybe this will stop your blubbering."

That card he knew was Hetty. A moment later she was with them in person, and Archie's bad humor vanished. There was something to a girl like Hetty—

"Well, what a cozy little threesome," she said smiling. "I don't know where we are or what this is all about, Archie, but lead on! We're with you!"

CHAPTER SIXTEEN
Two Camera Flashes

"MAYBE you two can figure an answer to this puzzle," said Archie. "I can't. I got in here by mistake. I was looking for someone and I lost the trail. Now we are 30 or 35 feet down in the earth. This tunnel leads into the side of the old well in the court. Here. I'll show you."

Archie beckoned to them with his flashlight. Hetty saw there was nothing to do but crawl along after him on her hands and knees. At first Grace would not go. The party stalled while she began complaining.

"Sorry I can't furnish hiking outfits," said Archie. "You'll have to make the best of it."

"This is revolting," said Grace. "It's absolutely against my principles."

Archie wished there were some convenient way to put Grace back into the book. "Come along. I'll have two witnesses to what I have seen here."

"You had no right to bring me down here this time of night," Grace whined.

"It's always night in a tunnel," said Archie. "What difference does it make?"

Grace demanded to know what time it was. Archie glanced at his watch. The hands pointed to a quarter after six. That was no help. His watch had gone dead hours ago.

Grace declared she would go back alone. She started off in the darkness, after Archie assured her that that was the direction he had come from. He and Hetty crept on toward the wall.

"How many flash bulbs do you have?"

"Several," said Hetty. "I'll keep the camera ready...oh, so this is the garden well."

The hollow shafts echoed below wisps of sound from somewhere overhead. The rustle of leaves, the voices at a little distance. The weird blend was worth listening to, and Hetty was fascinated. Some people were in the garden, but their conversation was indistinct.

Presently these sounds were drowned by the wail of Grace. Archie turned the flashlight around. The frightened girl was coming back, brushing the sides of the tunnel, heedless of her clothes.

"I thought she wouldn't go far alone," Hetty whispered, "but we'd better get her back right away."

"As soon as we get a picture or two," said Archie.

Grace did not bother to explain her sudden return, but she was in a troublesome mood. "You've got to take me back. You've no right to keep me down here."

"If you'll just be patient—"

"Is that the garden well?" Grace's eyes lost some of their fright as an idea dawned. "Then it's easy. All we have to do is call. Someone will let a ladder down for us."

Without any hesitation Grace acted upon this inspiration. She started to cry out. Instantly Archie dropped his flashlight and cupped his hands over her mouth.

"No! That won't do. There's someone up there—"

Grace tried to fight out of his grip. She mumbled, "Keep your hands off me or I'll scream."

It took Hetty's tact to quiet her.

"She doesn't understand, Archie. If it's dangerous for us to call to someone, then we won't call. All you have to do is explain. We're ready to help you."

Then the two girls sat quietly, waiting for Archie to explain his mysterious caution.

"Take my word for it, those voices up there mean trouble. Listen to them…one of them is Marcus Drake."

"Marcus Drake—" Hetty's tone conveyed a great deal.

THE name meant nothing to Grace. As Archie talked he turned off the flashlight. The voices overhead were coming closer. Archie's narrative—the strange dream of a few nights before—came forth in slow, broken phrases. Through the spaces of silence he could hear the echoing voice of Marcus Drake, a fitting accompaniment to his story.

"I'd better not tell you the last of it," said Archie, "but I'm convinced of this: Drake has been hurling his victims into this well. I'm sure of it. And yet I can't prove it. For an hour I have tried to fish a body out of that black water. It's only about 5 feet deep. But I couldn't find a thing."

"It must have been a dream," said Grace.

"But I've seen Marcus Drake at work," said Hetty. "I'm ready to believe—"

The overhead voices were now louder, more distinct in tone. Marcus Drake's guest was telling a funny story.

By bending through the opening and resting his shoulders on the edge of the brick wall, Archie could look up at the dark sky and see silhouetted there within the circle the two black knobs which were the heads of Drake and his guest. Hetty wanted to see, too.

Perhaps the eagerness of a candid camera expert becomes great enough to outweigh even the instinct of self-preservation. Perhaps Hetty's habits functioned against her will. The camera clicked and flashed.

Archie never knew what he uttered. In that second of surprise he was not sure whether it was a camera or a gun. He only knew he must jerk Hetty back into the tunnel before she fell headlong into the well. This he did, wasting no tenderness in the action.

He jerked her back *before she could be struck by the falling body.*

At the very split second of the flash, it seemed, the overhead talk had been broken off by a choking, grating sound, as of blades cutting into cartilage. A body was falling.

"Get back!" Archie snapped. "Get back out of my way!"

He barely touched the flashlight switch. The brief glow showed him the location of the hook he had used. At the same time he saw the water splashing high. The body had struck like a crack of close thunder. And now the echoes of the splash were rolling away through the hollow spaces.

Archie gathered the rope in his left hand, caught the wire hook in his right.

This time he couldn't miss. He hadn't seen the body actually fall, but he knew the murdered man was there in the water a few feet below him. Now there would be time—

Why did that water keep splashing?

"Hetty! The flash!"

Hetty obeyed the order in her own way. All Archie wanted was a flashlight beam to direct him as he threw the hook. What he got was another flash of the camera. What he saw almost paralyzed him.

The bottom of the well, it seemed, was suddenly rising. It was a wide metal disc with a beveled edge, and some system of levers was pushing it upward from the under side, like a piston in a cylinder. The water was spilling down on all sides of it. On its surface lay the immersed and bloody mass of clothes and flesh that was Marcus Drake's latest victim.

Even in the brief flash of the camera Archie saw that the false bottom of the well being thrust upward was turning on the vertical arm that supported it from the under side. It was turning to dump its load into the unknown depth of the shaft.

CHAPTER SEVENTEEN
A Ghost in a Jam.

ARCHIE lashed out with the hook and it caught. The falling weight threw him forward, but he flattened against the floor of the tunnel and held on for dear life. The prize was his and he pulled it in, hand over hand.

"The flashlight, Hetty. It's under my feet. Give me a light here, but don't turn it toward the well."

"What was it, Archie?" Hetty was gasping. "It looked like a dummy."

"A dummy with his throat cut. I've got him here. I'm dragging him in over the wall. Get back, Grace. Give me a light, Hetty. He's about to slip outa my hands...wait, I'm okay now. Never mind the light."

Grace was sobbing now and Hetty tried to silence her. In the pitch darkness neither of the girls could quite realize what had happened. But things were clearing up for Archie.

He knew he had acted in the nick of time. He knew that this was not a well, it was a chute for the disposing of murdered men. Undoubtedly the shaft led down to make contact with the deep storm-sewer that led to the lake.

"Quiet, you two. Listen. Drake's talking. He sounds worried. Those two flashes of light—"

"I know I shouldn't have taken those pictures," Hetty whispered. "He couldn't help seeing. He'll know we're down here."

"Quiet! ...Hear that? He saw *red.*"

From the low mumblings of Marcus Drake, conferring with his two henchmen, Archie was not convinced that the murderer knew what had happened. Rather, it sounded as if this deadly act always gave Drake a momentary hallucination of "seeing red" and this time he "saw fire once or twice."

"Not gettin' weak knees, are you, Boss?" came Mac's taunt.

"Weak knees, hell!" Drake growled bitterly. "It was that bad liquor I got at the tavern...or it might have been something else, now that I think of it."

"Where you goin', Boss?"

"Never mind me. Get that garden hose into action and wash up the stains. And be sure you run plenty of water in the well...and don't let me hear any more blab about weak knees. I'd like to see you slit a throat. You'd probably get mixed up and cut your own."

All of these words might have been spoken in voices that were scarcely more than whispers, but the cylindrical walls carried them perfectly. Again Grace began to whimper.

"Quiet!" Archie snapped. "Our lives aren't worth a nickel if they find out what we've got on them. But if they don't find out, we got the goods that'll hang them all."

His talk only terrified Grace, and as her sobbing faded away into silence he knew that she was turning into a card.

"Are you still with me, Hetty?" he whispered. "I didn't mean to make you go through all this—"

"Don't mind me, Archie. You've got the goods on them all right. You're taking a long chance, but your nerves are getting tougher."

He understood. He hadn't forgotten that during their first eaves dropping adventure he had acted boldly because of Hetty. Even now, as he dragged the murdered body a little farther back into the tunnel, it was her presence that made him conscious of his daring.

He found the flashlight and turned its sickly orange glow on the bloody, water-soaked form. He recognized the face of the man he had seen in the tavern a few days before. The muscular neck was bowed, half closing the gash in the windpipe. Archie's blood chilled at the sight. He turned the flashlight off, but kept thinking of Whiskey Phil's description; the fellow would thrust his head forward like a snake when he sprang the point of a funny story.

A FEW moments ago this fellow had been in the midst of a story. Just now the two men at the top of the well were mentioning that fact, and Mac was muttering disconsolately because Marcus Drake hadn't let the guy finish. "Damn it, we never will get the end of that story."

"You'd better get to work with that garden hose." Drake's voice trailed off as though he was leaving the garden area.

"I never saw him act so worried before," another voice continued. "He's so damned egotistical he thinks he's takin' no risks. Just because nobody'll ever find a body in this well—"

The voices faded out of hearing range. Presently there were sounds of the hose stream shooting against the rock railing. Splashes of water came chasing down the walls. Soon the well was refilling.

"We'll have to wait right here, Hetty, until they—Hetty, are you here?"

"Sorry, Archie," came a low gasp. "That sight was too much...I'm passing out."

"Gee, I'm sorry. But I'll take care of you, Hetty. You know you mean everything—"

Archie broke off, a little surprised at what he was saying. He doubted whether she heard. By this time she had become a card, waiting to be packed away in his book. It was just as well. Getting out of this hole was going to be difficult enough for one. It would be much worse for three. He groped for the flashlight, intending to pick up the two cards and deposit them in his book.

He found only one card.

He combed the walls and floor looking for the other one.

He rolled the dead man over, thinking that a card might have slipped into the heap of wet clothing. The card wasn't to be found. In desperation he even searched the ceiling. No card.

However, he noticed something that had previously escaped him. There was a shelf overhead that might have been cut for the storage of tools. For the narrow space of about a yard, the ceiling of the tunnel was formed of three wide planks planted crosswise, and a narrow opening had been left in front of these to give access to the storage space above them.

The little overhead cavern proved to be empty. Archie shrugged and returned to the business of searching for the lost card.

Could it be that one of the girls had not reverted to the card form, but had retreated through the tunnel?

Archie acted on this hunch. He followed the tunnel back toward the pit, studying the tracks carefully. By the time he reached the low ledge of stone that had given him the tight squeeze he was certain that no one but himself had passed this way.

At this point sounds filtered through from the pit where he had descended. Sounds of hammering. So Marcus Drake had suspected something! And now he was at the top of the pit, no doubt, mending the broken ladder.

That changed Archie's plans completely. No more patient waiting for the men to finish up and knock off for the night. It was high time for him to find a way out of here—for his own sake and the sake of the card he held in his hand.

He hurried back to the well. The hose was still spilling down the wall. The voices were droning on, recounting some of the stories that the latest victim had told. Presently Mac was again grumbling over Drake's failing to wait for the point of the last story.

Archie cupped his hands to his mouth. He called out in a weird, mournful voice:

"Come on down and I'll finish the story."

THE mumble of voices from overhead became quieted whispers. Mac was sure that call had been for him. Krug refused to believe his ears.

"It *couldn't* be. Dead men don't talk. Besides, he's gone on down by this time."

Archie gave out with another low moan. Then, summoning his best "otherworldly" voice he called out to the two men above, "Listen to me…both of you. I'll give you the finish of that story you love so much. And then I'll go. I'll go away and leave you alone. But you have to do me a favor in return."

"It's him!" Krug gasped. "He wants us to do something. He's still alive."

"It's him, all right, but he's dead," Mac declared. "You can tell it by his voice. I've heard of this kinda thing before. My old granny used to tell me all about dead spirits. He's comin' back—comin' back to make trouble. I been afraid o' this all along."

The two men listened incredulously. Slowly Archie's instructions carried up to them. "You must now act quickly," he said, his ghostly commands echoing up the well shaft. "I'm coming back for Marcus Drake. I don't care about the two of you—so long as you help me. But Drake…I must have him. I must find Marcus Drake. I *will* find Marcus Drake. And the two of you will help me. You must act quickly, though. Find a long ladder and lower it into this well… *now!*"

As Archie listened to the nervous reactions to his demands, his hopes rose and fell by turns. The men wanted to run, but they dared not. They wanted to report to Marcus Drake, but Archie gave them a ghostly warning to forestall that. He would stand for no delays, and if they wanted to be spared his haunting—

"We got you," said Mac. "Krug'll get the ladder right away."

"And you," Archie called, "you stay where you are...Mac. I need your company. When the ladder is lowered, I want you both to come down here...I've something to show you before I finish the story you're so anxious to hear the conclusion to..."

Archie took this precaution for fear he would never recover his ghostly grip upon these two if they both got out of the range of his voice.

In a few minutes the ladder was dangling down the inside of the wall. Archie could hear the two men immediately descending.

His plan was simple. He had dragged the body of the murdered man several feet into the tunnel so that the curving walls hid it from the opening into the well. That would enable him to hide on the shelf while the men followed the tunnel beyond him. When they came upon the body, he would have a clear path to the ladder.

He barely had time to ascend the shelf, which was well concealed from their direction. He called to them once more. "Come back this way. I'm waiting for you in the tunnel."

Now he could hear them struggling to cross from the end of the ladder into the tunnel opening. Bright rays of a flashlight swept the floor beneath him. Presently they came, trailing along on hands and knees—Mac with a flashlight, Krug with a pistol.

"Damndest thing I ever heard of," Krug whispered.

"It just goes to show you," said Mac, "that Drake should've let him finish that story. His ghost can't rest easy till he gets it told."

"Drake don't know everything," Krug muttered. "We sure as hell won't tell him about this."

"Listen!" Mac stopped short. "Thought I heard someone stompin' around."

The two men proceeded cautiously. They were ten feet beyond Archie now. A little farther and it would be safe—

But they came to a dead stop. From their vantagepoint they could undoubtedly see the figure of the murdered man in their path. Mac turned the flashlight back and forth along the walls. He spoke in a voice that was choked with fear.

"Well, here we are."

The walls gave back no answer, and Mac and Krug exchanged uncertain glances.

"I dunno 'bout this," said Krug. "I can't figure out how he got back here—unless Drake didn't do a good job of it."

"He looks awful dead," Mac whispered. Then he raised his voice in another effort to connect with the spirit. "Are you here? Where'd you go?"

"Ssssh! I *did* hear somethin'. Someone's comin' through the tunnel."

ARCHIE'S chance had never come. Now he was on the verge of making a dash, but just as he started to climb down from the shelf the two men began backing down the path toward him. He hovered at the edge of the plank and held his breath. "Cover your light," Krug was saying.

Then Archie saw that another faint glow was approaching. The two men were paralyzed with the uncertainty of their situation. Would the approaching ghost carry a light? Of course not. They wanted to retreat, but they were afraid of disobeying that voice.

The approaching light burst full in their faces and the guttural voice of Marcus Drake barked at them.

"Why, you damned dirty double-crossers!"

CHAPTER EIGHTEEN
Elevator Going Down

MARCUS M. DRAKE was almost too mad to speak. Archie would not have been the least bit surprised if he had opened fire with his brand new pistol, if only to kick up some dust at his henchmen's heels.

Like a pair of punctured balloons the two henchmen began to sputter and puff and cough. Together they succeeded in putting across exactly nothing. Their stammerings about ghosts and voices glanced off their steel-tempered boss like drops of water off a brick wall.

"Dirty double-crossers," was about all that Drake could utter. He was appalled to think that such inferior thugs would dare to sidetrack one of his carefully dispatched victims. There could be only one reason for their doing such a thing, he decided—they meant to give him the works and run out on him.

"Honest, boss, we never dreamed of such a thing. Shoot us dead if you want to, but I swear to high heaven—" Krug was begging for mercy.

"You got us all wrong," Mac couldn't hold the flashlight still, and his free hand was pressing against his sagging jaw. "He ain't dead, boss. He was *callin'* to us. He made us come down, honest."

Marcus Drake kicked at the corpse.

"He's as dead as your dead brains. How'd he get into this tunnel? Not by himself."

"He called us in here. *That's* where we found him."

"You're talking like idiots," Drake snarled. "Who's down here besides you?"

"I dunno," said Krug. "We only got this far when we heard you comin' toward us. Is there someone else down here? We never passed no one. Did you?"

Drake disliked being thrown on the defensive, and he checked his impulse to glance back over his trail. "If there's anybody working with you hams, he's on your side of the body, not mine. I've just cleared the tunnel, and nobody got by me."

"We came down through the well," said Mac weakly. "Nobody got by us."

"I think I got it figured out," said Krug. "Someone on top musta threw his voice down the well."

"Very likely," said Drake sarcastically. "And it scared the corpse into jumpin' into the tunnel—right. That smoothes out everything, don't it? Except why the hell the body didn't shoot-the-shoots on down to the storm sewer. Explain that, can you? I know damn well I pressed the button, and I heard the water carry off."

"You can't blame us for that trouble, boss. We was up here with you then. Remember, you walked off."

"Well...maybe."

"Hey, what gave you the idea of comin' down here?" Mac saw he was on the trail of something now, and his voice stiffened into accusation. "By George, you musta knew you'd slipped off with your shears. You came down to check up."

Krug followed through. "Then he *was* alive."

"He was dead," Drake snapped.

"Then he's still hauntin' us," said Mac, shrinking back from the body.

Marcus Drake muttered uneasily to himself then gave his thugs new orders. "Drag him to the well. I'll take your flashlight. There, move him along."

As the party passed beneath Archie, Drake missed bumping his head on the planks by a fraction of an inch. Another moment and one of the three might become cognizant of his hiding place. Archie made ready to slip down. He didn't straighten his clothes, though he felt sure that the rope and hook lumped between his ribs and the shelf was tangled up with his coat.

Darkness was in his favor for the moment. It was all a matter of timing. With the splash of the body into the well Archie bounded down and raced through the tunnel toward the pit. On hands and knees he ran, his shoulder brushing the walls to guide him.

ALREADY the light had turned, and its dim glow seeped around the curve. Then Archie was ahead of it, into the welcome blackness again. But the rumbling of voices had suddenly gone quiet, and Archie knew the men were listening. His thudding hands and knees had made too much noise. He cut his speed, slipped along as noiselessly as he could.

This sharp curve he remembered. Just ahead he would run into the narrow passage under the low ceiling of rock. If he could get through it undiscovered—

"Who's there?" Drake's voice rolled through the tunnel like thunder. "Who's there?" The voice was coming closer. So was the light.

Archie turned and backed into the narrows. If they crowded down on him he would be facing the right direction. The pistol with the corrugated handle was in his hand.

He fought his way backward. But he wouldn't make it. They were just around the sharp bend now.

"Who's there?" came the challenging snarl.

Archie gave back in a voice that would have chilled the gods of death. "I'm looking—for—Marcus—Drake!"

"Who the devil is that?"

"I—passed—over—him—once—but—this—time...I'll *get* him."

"Like hell you'll get me!" Drake sneered. Archie could see his shadow forging ahead of the flashlight. He must have been on his knees and one hand; the shadow of his gun arm moved steadily along the wall. The gun came in sight at the turn, its short barrel glistening. There it stopped.

Archie held his breath and waited. He could hear Drake whispering to his men to come closer. The party fell silent as if waiting for another call from the unknown voice. Archie wouldn't give them the satisfaction. Another step and they would discover him. Then gunfire would do the bidding of Fate.

The shadow moved. The gun hand became an arm and shoulder, the broad cheekbone and narrowed eye and bulldog jaw of Marcus Drake. His twisted lips whispered something. Archie thought he was calling for more light.

Archie's fingered tightened. He was about to shout something, but Drake hadn't seen him yet. And then, suddenly, a strange something happened that turned Drake's head.

A voice called, "Whoo-oo-oo-ooo...where are you?"

It might have come from the well. At least from somewhere back in the curved passage that Marcus Drake and his party had just covered.

"There," came Krug's low voice. "I told you so."

"It came from this way before," Drake growled.

"Now maybe you'll believe us," said Mac. "This damned place is haunted..."

"Sounded to me like a female; maybe spirits sound that way when they're in pain."

"It's a trick," said Drake. "Come on. Ten to one we'll find someone crawlin' the ladder."

The three men turned back. Archie followed them. It made no difference now that he had a clear course for an escape. His responsibility was plain. That voice was the girl he had lost—he wasn't sure which one.

Or was it? His hand plunged to his coat pocket. The book was hanging like a flap. What had caused that? The leap from the shelf? He had been in a tangle with the rope and hook. The one card must have spilled out and come to life.

He synchronized his creeping steps with the thud of Mac's hands and knees, and kept barely in sight of the retreating figures. Another call from the girl had urged them on. The round echoes of her voice left Archie still uncertain which girl. But the fact that she was calling—not sobbing or shrieking in terror—led him to believe it must be Hetty.

"By George, it is a female," he heard Drake declare. "And a damned good looker. Am I seeing things?

Hello, there. What the devil are *you* doing down here?"

ARCHIE couldn't see her. Evidently Drake and the others could. But not for long. Archie heard her utter a little cry of astonishment. That was all. Then there was only the baffled gasping of Mac and Krug and the dumbfounded growl of Marcus Drake.

"Where's she going? Keep your light steady there. She's trying to get away."

"She's turning invisible," Krug said in an awe-stricken voice.

"It's a trick!" Marcus Drake snapped, as if that assertion made him the master of the situation.

It was a trick, all right. Archie had suspected, from his conversations with Hamilton Craig, that this miracle of science was one of the secrets that Dr. Silverhead had never shared with anyone else. Now Archie could see with his own eyes how completely mystified were these onlookers.

The girl must have completely disappeared before their eyes. Marcus Drake felt impelled to explain what had happened. His two satellites must be convinced this was no spirit, but only a trick.

"She's covered herself in some invisible wrap. No, don't shoot. Keep close against the walls so she can't slip through you. She'll make a break for the ladder in the well."

"Which way do we go, Boss?"

"Right up after her. She'll not get far with this."

Archie took the precaution to hold back while the three men crossed from the mouth of the tunnel onto the hanging ladder. None of them stopped to notice the white card that had fallen into the dust.

Archie stored the card in the leather book and carefully pinned it in his pocket.

Again he shot a hasty glance around the premises, but the second card was not to be found.

His recent pursuers were still ascending when the daring inspiration struck him. He would still rescue that body. What could more certainly baffle and convict them?

No time to waste fishing from the surface with a rope and hook. With supreme determination he let himself down over the brick wall into the chilly water. The descent was made with almost complete silence.

Low splashes accompanied his attempt to locate the submerged form with his feet. From high overhead came someone's savage assertion that that damned spirit had bypassed them again.

Drake retorted that they'd shine a light down as soon as they made the rail.

Which meant that Archie had seconds to go. He located the limp form, locked his arms under the chest, and drew the weight up through the surface of the water.

Then it happened—swiftly, inescapably.

The bottom of the well thrust upward, hurling Archie off his balance. It tipped to one side. The water became a waterfall. And Archie and the body of the murdered man plummeted down into a pitch-black oblivion.

CHAPTER NINETEEN
The Craigettes Carry On

BY THE following evening the affairs at the mansion were becoming badly disorganized. For the first day and a half, three Craigettes had been carrying on without any supervision. Hamilton Craig had not been seen. Moreover, his lieutenant, Archie Burnette, had mysteriously disappeared.

To make matters worse, three of the six usherettes could not be accounted for. Perhaps they were in Archie's book, perhaps they were lost; or—and this was a matter of much speculation and worry—perhaps they were out on conquests of their own.

From their first entrance through these doors Cornelia and Genevieve had sensed a personal jealousy over Hamilton Craig. The passing days had intensified these feelings. And now, when the girls should have been concerned over the personal safety of their missing companions, they were in reality disturbed by this jealous fire. Were Patsy and Grace and Hetty in the company of Hamilton Craig, or were they with Archie, whose word carried such great influence with the bachelor architect?

Cornelia, Genevieve, and Linda Lee did not openly quarrel about this problem, but each had set about strengthening her own campaign of conquest.

If Craig should come back tonight or tomorrow, he would discover some pronounced personality changes.

Cornelia was following her hunch that what this wealthy architect needed was a wife with a strong instinct for business. During the absence of her superiors she had taken personal command. She had declared the Craigette uniforms *passe* and had donned a tailored business suit, which gave her the air of a woman executive. She monopolized the reception desk, determined to run up a record of rental contracts before Craig's return.

However, Cornelia's high-pressure tactics had worked adversely, and by the evening she could not deny that business was bad.

Cornelia was checking over the books when Genevieve came down. Genevieve was wearing pink. She might have been dressed for a party—a long flowing pink gown, a pink rose in her hair, pink slippers.

The lounge lizards, Verrazzano and Whiskey Phil, eyed her with approval as she crossed to Cornelia's desk.

Cornelia's eyes flashed a soft jealous fire. "I suppose you think that should be the new Craigette uniform?"

"I'm going out with Mr. Dodge," said Genevieve haughtily. "Anything to kill the evening. Business is so dull around here." Her eyes lingered a little too long on Cornelia's bookkeeping figures. But she tossed her head in the air and started off as if business matters were beneath her contempt. Cornelia called her back.

"Your weekly check. And you needn't stare at it. You see—" Cornelia jotted some figures with a pencil. "I have made a slight deduction for the Craigette Protection Fund. You haven't heard of it? It's my own invention. Each girl will contribute. The fund will be useful when we land bigger contracts and tour the country with a show."

"And who takes care of the money?" Business matters were no longer beneath Genevieve's contempt.

"Leave that to me. I'll invest it—and not in pink slippers."

The brickbats were beginning to fly when Benjamin Dodge arrived, breaking up the quarrel. Genevieve was glad enough to be rescued even though she made it plain to her escort that she was really much too aristocratic to be associating with him.

A FEW minutes later a young bond salesman came to call on Cornelia, and Carlo Verrazzano threatened to walk out in a huff. "So long have I waited for the beautiful Cornelia…"

Cornelia had her own strategy. She called her two gentlemen friends into conference and then added Whiskey Phil to the circle and conferred with all three of them. The Craigette Protection Fund must be used to insure the welfare of the six usherettes.

"Body guards will be needed," said Cornelia, "brave, strong men. Men who will be ready to answer any emergency call."

The bond salesman frowned and picked up his briefcase. "I guess I'm not going to be available for your little games. Furthermore, I suspect that you girls are quite capable of taking care of yourselves without us."

"Three of us have disappeared," countered Cornelia.

"Then I suggest you call the police," said the bond salesman, "unless these two gentlemen are the brave strong bodyguards you are looking for. Good evening."

The door slammed and Cornelia was left with her two doubtful applicants. She decided to adjourn the conference. She had work to do. Whiskey Phil took the hint and floated off toward the nearest bar. Verrazzano rolled his eyes and began cooing about a moon that was due to rise in another hour or two. Cornelia asked him to leave the house.

It might have been a peaceful evening for Cornelia if she could have spent it filling a scratch pad with dollar signs and figures with lots of zeros. But presently Linda Lee intruded upon her solitude.

"Don't tell me," said Cornelia, "that you've been over at the doctor's laboratory again."

"Isn't he the most fascinatin' puhson?" said Linda. "He talks in such big words, and I can't undahstand a thing he says. He's really mahvelous."

Cornelia shrugged. She had little in common with this giddy Southern girl who knew nothing at all about business.

But tonight, to Cornelia's surprise, Linda Lee dropped a remark that had the right ring to it. "If the doctor's invention was successful it would make a fortune for someone." For whom? Linda Lee did not know. Why didn't she ask? Because the doctor never answered her questions anyway. He just went on talking.

"How big a fortune?"

"Oh, a few million, I guess," Linda Lee answered carelessly. "Where is everybody, Cornelia? Isn't there any excitement around here tonight?"

"Plenty of excitement," said Cornelia, "if you have the wits to see it. Where did you leave the doctor? Come on, you're taking me over to see him."

Linda Lee led the way through the mansion. She didn't think the doctor would be very sociable, since he was still busy grinding a lens. But if Cornelia insisted—

Cornelia stopped and caught Linda Lee by the arm. Someone was coming up the rear of the walk, *limping*.

Into the light of the rear porch came Patsy. She clutched the rail of the steps for support. Her Oriental costume was bedraggled, her red hair in disarray, her wrist was bleeding. But as always, her eyes glowed with belligerence.

"Mah goodness!" Linda Lee gasped. "Did y'all get hit by a freight train?"

"I fell—damn it!" said Patsy. "Where's Craig? Has he come back?"

"He's been missing for two days," said Cornelia, helping Patsy to a chair. "Where on earth have you been? Where did you fall from?"

"That," said Patsy, "I wouldn't know. I was a card when I started falling, but I was me when I landed."

CHAPTER TWENTY
The Man with the Beard

THE clerk in the novelty store on Fourteenth Street scrutinized his masterpiece with satisfaction.

"There, you see. No false face was necessary, sir. Your best friends won't know you now. I have changed the shape of your mustache, I've added spectacles, a goatee and triangular eyebrows."

The subject appraised himself in a mirror. "A very good job. Of course my tallness—but I can't expect you to change that."

"As long as you're wearing that coat, sir, the padding alters your build. Now if your walk doesn't give you away, I'm sure you are perfectly disguised."

The customer stroked his goatee, as though already fond of it. He paid his bill and walked out with a confident step.

BY THE time Patsy had acquired three or four bandages she decided to speak up and tell what had happened. Linda Lee was massaging her injured ankle. Cornelia was trying to make her keep the thermometer in her mouth. And Genevieve, recently returned from an evening with Benjamin Dodge, stopped by, trying to remain aloof.

"Don't you dare call the police," said Patsy for the fifth time. "Hamilton told me there might be some trouble, but it's his own private fight."

"She calls him Hamilton," said Grace.

"Here's how it happened." Patsy took a deep breath. "We were going to take in the midnight revue, Hamilton and I. As we were going down the walk to his car, those two night watchmen fell in with us. One of them said, 'Give us a ride down the street, pal,'—but Hamilton said, 'Nothing doing.' They were supposed to be on duty here. So one of them, the tall one with the crooked nose, started swearing for no reason at all. Then he said, 'If you won't take us riding, we'll take *you* for one.' The next thing I knew they were fighting. The tall guy tried to pull a gun, and then Ham knocked it out of his hand."

"She calls him Ham," said Genevieve.

"When it comes to a good fight," Patsy continued, "I always forget to faint the way a lady is supposed to. They thought I was running away, but I wasn't. I was heading for the pile of bricks the builders had left by the walk. My bare fists are not much good, and when I skipped a brick off that tall bird's head, he figured I was worth a left to the jaw. Next thing I knew I was turning into thin air, hoping Hamilton would remember to pick me up, though I knew the chances were two to one they would kayo him."

"Mah goodness!" said Linda Lee. "That's a lot of fightin' over a cah ride."

"Don't be stupid," said Cornelia. "There's some feud that we don't know about. We've got to keep this out of the papers. Business is bad enough."

"I woke up just once during these last forty-eight hours," Patsy went on. "What I found made me so fighting mad that I turned right back into a card. Ham was beside me, bound and gagged. We were in an empty room, somewhere high up. He had rescued me from the fight, all right, and I imagine he had worked a long time to get me out of his pocket."

"So you came to life and untied him?" Cornelia asked.

"I came to life and should have untied him, but I was such a chicken-livered weakling—it makes me furious to think of it—of all the luck! Just as I started to work on the ropes, we heard the two thugs coming up the stairs. Hamilton told me to hide, but darn it—I passed into thin air again."

"I don't blame you," said Linda Lee.

"The next thing I knew I was floating down past the hospital wall, coming back to myself. I landed with an awful bounce on this ankle, and here I am."

"And where," asked Genevieve, "is our Hamilton?"

"That's what I'm going to find out," said Patsy, her lips tightening. "He's probably in one of the third floor rooms behind a locked door."

Obviously the thing to do was to rescue Hamilton Craig.

Patsy was ready, willing, and almost able. She tried her weight on her bandaged ankle and said, "That'll do. All I need is a reliable weapon. Are you girls with me?"

"I've just contributed to a protective agency," said Genevieve. "Personally I don't care for brawls. Cornelia may have my share."

"Down where Ah come from," said Linda Lee, "the men folks are always glad to do the fighting."

Patsy turned to Cornelia as her one hope in this emergency. Cornelia feigned a willingness to attack the problem vigorously. However, she believed everything should be talked over thoroughly before plunging ahead. It would be well to find out where the two burly night watchmen were spending the evening before invading their territory. And what about the lights that would go on automatically whenever a person passed from one room to another? And what about a choice of witnesses in case this action should eventually end up in a court of law?

THE more Cornelia talked, the angrier Patsy became. "I don't give a darn about your ifs and ands and whereases. Our job is to find Hamilton Craig and cut those ropes. Are you with me or aren't you?"

The telephone rang in Craig's office. Genevieve was glad of the chance to escape.

"Are you with me, Cornelia?" Patsy shot her challenge squarely.

"I'm with you, but I'm not going to lose my temper about it. You're too hotheaded, Patsy. If you hadn't started throwing bricks—"

"Oh, so it's all *my* fault. *I'm* the one who tied him into knots. I could use a few bricks right now."

Cornelia tried to calm her. "Linda Lee is right, we need some men to help us. I have just been talking with Carlo Verrazzano and—"

"Verrazzano!"

Patsy did begin throwing things. All of Cornelia's precious bookkeeping ledgers began to fly.

It was Genevieve's telephone conversation that brought a hush over the group. The call evidently came from Hamilton Craig's office—at this time of night! Someone was coming out to investigate Craig's strange absence. He should arrive in a few minutes.

"There," said Cornelia, "I told you we shouldn't be too hasty."

It was precisely midnight when the doorbell rang and the three girls found themselves face to face with a stranger of most striking appearance. Tall, heavy shouldered, most dignified in bearing, he did not look to be a man accustomed to dealing with situations of violence. But his eyes were keen and he was surprisingly young to be wearing a gray goatee.

He took a step into the reception room, bowed with a flourish, and said, "I'm very much concerned about Hamilton Craig. I'm his best friend. In fact, I have known him all my life. I understand that he has not been seen for the past forty-eight hours. If any of you ladies can assist me—"

He paused, and his eyes were intent upon Patsy, who was waving at him with a bandaged wrist.

"I've just been elected," said Patsy. "Follow me!"

CHAPTER TWENTY-ONE
H.C. and Hamilton Craig

PATSY was temporarily on her good behavior. She felt constrained to keep her temper under control in the presence of this tall man who reminded her so much of Hamilton Craig. She felt somewhat restored as a result of first-aid treatment and a cup of hot tea. It was good to be in fresh, comfortable clothes again. Linda Lee had loaned her a starchy white slack suit, which went well with her red hair. The tall man's approving glances told her so.

He was older than Hamilton Craig by ten or fifteen years, she guessed, but he had the same energetic manner, curiously tinged with shyness.

It was evident that he knew much about Hamilton Craig. Secret knowledge had obviously been shared with him, such as how to cut off the lights that would otherwise pop on automatically when anyone walked through the rooms. Patsy expressed her surprise at this. The tall man did not hesitate to reveal these confidences.

"Craig meant this lighting device to control the comings and goings of a lot of scoundrels who have been nesting in these old empty buildings. But from the way things have gone, the trick wasn't very successful."

"Maybe Mr. Craig hired the wrong men as night watchmen," Patsy suggested.

"Do you think so?"

"Aren't they the same scoundrels you were talking about, Mr.—?"

"Just call me H.C.," said the tall man. "Those are my initials."

The surprising thing was that they were the initials of Hamilton Craig. Patsy mentioned this to him.

"We are related," H.C. said lightly. "Those initials run in the family."

Patsy accepted the explanation. It helped her understand the similarities between these two men—the expression of the eyes, the manner of walking, even the tone of the voice.

They ascended to the second floor, passed through a wing of newly decorated apartments, came to a stop near the middle of the building, where the plasterers' equipment blocked the stairs. Patsy was almost certain the prisoner was in a third floor room.

To her surprise H.C. picked her up and lifted her over the barricade of plasterers' supplies, and set her down on the third step.

"So we won't leave any white tracks on the stairs," he explained.

They reached the top step. He drew her arm through his and they started down the line of rooms.

"I don't think Mr. Craig is interested in any girls," said Patsy. "And I don't blame him, the way all of us sit around talking about him."

"Oh, they do? What do they say?"

"What they say makes no difference to me," said Patsy.

At the end of the corridor they turned back. They had glanced into each room not already occupied by tenants.

"I must be wrong," Patsy said. "But I remember distinctly it was an empty room, with yellow walls and a crack in the plaster that looked like a falling palm tree. And there was one window."

"Facing the court or the street?"

"The court, I think. I was too mad to see straight. You see I had just woke up when we heard the men coming up the stairs."

"Then the room must be near a stairway."

H.C. led her back to the center of the building.

"We didn't try this room," said H.C., scrutinizing an obstructed doorway. "I'll move a few of these window frames and we'll see what's back here."

Patsy gave him a mocking smile. She thought he was being very impractical, and her patience and good behavior were wearing thin.

WHEREVER Hamilton Craig might be imprisoned, she felt sure it wouldn't be behind a doorway that was blocked by half a ton of floor lumber and a couple dozen window frames. If she knew those two night watchmen, they weren't the sort to relish work. And yet she was certain that they were obliged to drop in on their prisoner often enough to keep him from starving.

"Sap," she said.

H.C. apparently didn't like being called a sap by comparative strangers. But upon weighing her argument he decided to move no more window frames. He stepped down off the bundles of quarter-sawed oak.

However, the slight joggle of the whole stack of material fascinated him and he gazed back at it curiously.

"Are those frames bearing any weight against the wall or aren't they?" he asked, squinting at the shadows. "We'll answer that problem before we go on."

"Do you divide or multiply?" said Patsy, sarcastically.

"And what about those bundles being a quarter inch off the floor?"

"They must be hypnotized. Are you looking for Hamilton Craig or aren't you?"

H.C. didn't answer. He was down on his hands and knees trying to see underneath the stack of material. He slipped his fingertips under the corner and pulled. The stack of material rolled away from the door without so much as the quiver of a window frame.

"I thought so," he said, more to himself than to Patsy. "That whole caboodle of stuff is on casters. Well, this door should give us what we're looking for."

Patsy followed him into the wedge of space. He turned the knob and the door opened.

"We'll leave the room light off," he said. "There'll be enough gleam through these window frames. And we'd better pull them back in place while we're at it."

"Yellow walls," Patsy whispered, "with cracks like a falling tree. This must be the place."

H.C. called into the darkness.

"Are you there, Ham Craig? This is your—your friend, H.C. We've come to get you, Patsy and I. Where—oh, here you are. They've knotted you up a bit...Patsy, a little more light. No, not the switch. Just open the door a little wider. That's good. I'll have these ropes cut in a minute."

Patsy heard the relieved sigh of the prisoner. Once his gag was removed he was quick to come to life.

"Ah—that's better. I've been looking forward to this. The other arm first, if you don't mind. It's still got some feeling. The left one's numb. Is that Patsy with you, or am I seeing red?"

"It's me," said Patsy. "Nice little date we had. You sure threw me a swell party—so much fun."

"You did the throwing," said Hamilton Craig, trying to loosen the rusty joints in his free arm. "The way you toss bricks you ought to have a job with a wrecking crew, or maybe the St. Louis Browns. You sure wrecked me."

"There you go again," Patsy said hotly. "I s'pose you're going to tell H.C. it was all my fault."

"You grazed me with that brick...don't you remember?" asked Craig, rising slowly to his feet, "just as I was bearing down on those thugs for a knockout—"

"Listen to him rave, H.C.," Patsy taunted. "Knockout? All right, my aim slipped and I spared 'em the trouble. We're lucky they didn't shoot us both."

"I don't deny that," said Craig, lifting a foot out of the ropes. "All I'm saying is, when you got careless with that brick—"

"You'd better not talk," Patsy said in a screechy voice. "A couple of hours ago you threw me out that window."

"How could I throw you out when my hands were tied?" Craig growled. "You think I haven't had plenty of trouble protecting you? Yesterday when you turned into a card and fell to the floor you practically signed your death warrant. If those suspicious guys had seen you they'd have thought you were an invisible message. They'd have torn you to bits. But I did some swift headwork. I rolled over and sat on you."

"Headwork," Patsy echoed. "I ought to slap you. How did you finally get me out the window?"

"Kicked you out—with both feet."

"A fine time of night you chose."

"I'd been trying all day. I knew you'd be halfway down to earth before you started to gather weight, and you wouldn't do any more than break a leg. But I did expect you to heave a couple of bricks through my window for a thank you."

"I didn't know which window," said Patsy. "Any more insults?"

CRAIG turned his conversation to the mysterious H.C.— a veritable double for the architect in height and voice and profile. H.C. was energetically massaging Craig's arms and shoulders. In the dim yellow light that filtered into the room it was not easy to distinguish these two men. If anything, H.C. was slower of speech, more reserved, less disturbed by the gangster business that was operating on the premises.

But H.C.'s attitude was far from one of complacency. If anything, he was more in a mood for decisive action than Hamilton Craig, whose overwrought emotions could be seen in his exaggeration of trifles.

H.C. suggested that he stop his verbal sparring with Patsy; that there would be a time to weigh the details of their previous scrap with the two night watchmen before a judge.

But Hamilton Craig, for some reason that didn't make sense to Patsy, made another uncomplimentary remark about her brick-throwing ability and added injury to insult by warning H.C. that all these things should be considered carefully by any man contemplating matrimony.

Contemplating matrimony? What did that have to do with Patsy? In full fury Patsy's temper exploded.

Instead of turning to a card as any other Craigette would have done under this much stress, she stormed to the door like a cyclone. She thrust the stacked floor and window materials out of her way, dashed through, and gave the stuff a final push—such a vigorous one that the echoes of clattering window frames and lumber accompanied her all the way down the stairs.

She got back to the reception room several minutes ahead of Craig and H.C.—by chance just in time to answer a telephone call. Here it was one o'clock in the morning and some drunken dope was trying to locate Archie Burnette.

CHAPTER TWENTY-TWO
Early Morning Spree

WHISKEY PHIL hung up and turned to the bartender.

" 'Stoo bad. Archie ain't in. Or if he was, zhey didn't wanta bring 'im to the phone. Nice guy, thish Archie. Ya know 'im?"

The bartender nodded—he'd seen Archie around.

"Well, you oughta git better 'quainted, like I did," said Phil. "Let 'im sock ya in the jaw once. Thash how I got t'know 'im. He shocked me in the jaw, jis' like this…"

Whiskey Phil threw a wide haymaker that unbalanced him and left him clinging to the bar at a forty-five degree angle. He crawled back onto the stool.

"I wuz gonna tell Archie all 'bout this practical joke. Guess I'll write 'im a letter…'stoo good to keep. Will ya give it to Archie? Don't get grabby…ain't got no letter wrote yet. Gimme a peesha paper, will ya? That a boy."

Whiskey Phil wrote painstakingly for the next thirty minutes, and then gave the bartender the letter and went on his way.

His way took him through the Craig building into the interior court. He weaved in and out of the arcade. He encountered each pillar with an attitude that it was a personal friend. There would then be a one-sided argument as to how he was to get past.

He stopped to mutter over the strangeness of the heap of electrical equipment that had been deposited on the walkway, preparatory to the rigging of electric lights in the court. The rolls of wire failed to give him any back talk and he was disappointed. He kicked at them, then he took from his pocket a pair of pruning shears.

He snapped the shears but could not succeed in catching the end of the wire. Everything was falling away from him. The pruning shears, however, gave him a reason to smile. He was a practical joker, the most amusing person in the world. He staggered down the walk snapping the shears. When he came to the door that led to Marcus Drake's basement he muttered a deeply satisfied "Aha…this is the playsh."

The door was locked. This was annoying. Whiskey Phil tried several windows. But it was the door to Dr. Silverhead's laboratory that admitted him. The lights were friendly and inviting, and for a moment he was almost swerved from his purpose.

The pruning shears were still snapping in his hands, and so he plodded through a dark room grumbling mildly as he bumped into sharp objects and at last located the basement stairs that led to Marcus Drake's garden tools.

"Here she ish, hangin' on this nail. All r—right, Mishter Drake, we'll trade. You c'n have this one—I'll take yours for a shooveneer."

Suiting the action to the word, Philip Parker stumbled away, patting the new prize with the palm of his hand.

Half way through the dark room he stopped to look back and laugh. He laughed until he needed a drink. There was a bottle in his left hip pocket, but the bottle and the souvenir pruning shears were too much to handle at once. The bottle dropped and shattered.

"*Sssssh!* Don't be wakin' nobody up. This mus' be Mishter Drake's night to shleep."

The lights of Dr. Silverhead's laboratory again beckoned him, and he decided it would be a good time to drop in for a social call. Maybe he would find Archie. He still wanted to tell Archie his little joke.

Dr. Silverhead was seated at a table peering into a microscope. He glanced up at the intruder without actually seeing him, and returned his eyes to his work. He was operating a wooden wheel as large as an automobile steering wheel, which caused the object beneath the microscope to creep slowly back and forth.

Whiskey Phil was in a wilderness of bright scientific paraphernalia, none of which he understood. But the focus of the lights around the table directed his attention to the eight-inch lens beneath the microscope. Phil tried to intrude upon the doctor's concentration with a brisk "Good evenin'! Ish a nishe evenin'." Three times he repeated his greeting.

Then his sociability flagged and he sat down on a bench to mutter to himself.

A wave from the doctor silenced him, and for the next half-hour he sat there watching. Abruptly Dr. Silverhead turned, removed his spectacles and stared at Whiskey Phil through feverishly bright eyes.

"Not a flaw in it. It is perfect." The white-haired man rose and came over to Whiskey Phil with precise steps.

WHISKEY PHIL offered another greeting with his favorite comment about the nice evening, which the doctor ignored. It would seem that this was a moment of great achievement in the life of the scientist. A wealth of magnificent words was rolling off his tongue, and Phil sensed that they were an expression of exultation. He was fascinated by the wangling of the doctor's sharp-pointed beard and he tried to nod his acceptance of all that was being said.

"But there's one possible error," the doctor was saying. "The fifth figure beyond the decimal point was blurred. It was either a six or an eight. As the completed lens stands it is perfect—for the *eight.*"

"For the eight," Whiskey Phil echoed, with a glimmer of understanding. "Eight *what?*"

"I will put it into operation at once," the doctor continued, "if it focuses successfully, the missing digit was an eight. If it fails, I shall resume the task of microscopic abrasions until the point of six is reached. Could anything be more logical?"

"Nothin'," said Whiskey Phil. "It is the clearesh, mosh logical logic I ever heard. What ya gonna do 'bout it?"

"Within a few minutes I will know," said the doctor, consulting his watch. "One living subject will prove the point. I will have the lens inserted within five minutes. The crucial test will follow at once."

"Thish…ish…gonna…be…good."

The doctor started to put on his spectacles, but for an intense moment he gazed at Whiskey Phil, now very much aware of this visitor's presence. "If you will just remain seated, sir, I shall be ready at once."

" 'Sall right, I'm in no hurry. I've got all night."

Whiskey Phil gestured with the pruning shears, but it occurred to him that they were best kept out of sight since they were such a valuable souvenir. He hid them away in his hip pocket.

A few minutes later he yielded to the doctor's suggestion that he climb the ladder to the pinnacle of a towering instrument. It was a dizzy climb. This massive pyramid of gleaming black tubes, crackling with electric sparks, rose out of a gaping rectangular hole in the floor. It had its base on a lower level—a stage with wings full of tattered old scenery. As Whiskey Phil neared the top of the ladder, he fancied himself an actor. He was 18 or 20 feet above the top of the proscenium arch when he reached the summit of his climb.

He turned and called down to the doctor. "Didn't think I'd make it, didya?"

"No time to waste, sir. The power is on full. Proceed as I instruct you. There is a slide before you. You are to enter it feet first."

"Good ol' slipper shlide. Ish jis' like school dayzh."

"Everything is ready," the doctor ordered. "Proceed."

The drunken man obediently hurled his weight into the metal chute. He gave a hilarious shout as he swished down into the mysterious pyramid out of sight.

Dr. Silverhead bounded down a stairway to the level of the stage. He pranced back and forth in front of two short "slipper slides" which extended out from the base of the pyramid.

For thirty seconds he watched those two chutes expectantly. Nothing came out. He waited a full minute, then nodded decisively and switched off the power.

"It should have been six," he said to himself. "Two more days of grinding."

CHAPTER TWENTY-THREE
A Lesson for Linda Lee

"BUT disintegration isn't at all complicated," said Dr. Silverhead, as he unfolded a scientific chart for the benefit of his audience of one. That one—Linda Lee—was the perfect audience. She listened attentively, rolled her large childlike eyes in astonishment, and understood absolutely nothing.

"Only two nights ago I disintegrated one of my subjects completely," the doctor continued. "The process requires less than twenty seconds. At the end of that time there is nothing left."

"How remarkable," said Linda Lee. "Did it hurt him?"

"Hurt is a trifling thing. What is hurt? A state of mind—always temporary. Exceedingly temporary in his case. Does an operation hurt? A little perhaps, but it's necessary if the patient is going to regain his health. And this hurt was necessary to make our desired gains in new realms of science. By this subject's sacrifice I proved that my new lens was two-thousandths of a point off. But now I have rectified that error."

"Oh!" Linda Lee gasped. "Does that mean he'll be all right?"

"He no longer has any positive existence. The matter of which he was composed has been disintegrated. If you'll notice the round dots on this chart—"

"They look like dollahs and nickels and pennies falling through the aih."

The doctor smiled.

"These dots represent the electrons which make up the atoms of matter, of which all physical substance is composed. This larger dot—"

"Speaking of dollahs," said Linda Lee, sliding off the subject of electrons, "what happened to this puhson's money when you disamputated him? "Did it come down one of those big spouts?"

"Those chutes are where I expected him—to reappear after he slid down into the top of the machine. If my lens had been perfect he would have been duplicated. *One* of him would have emerged through each chute."

"One of him?"

"This machine, once I have it functioning properly again, will make duplicates of anything—living or dead."

"I worked in an office once," said Linda Lee, "and we used carbon paper for duplicates."

"This process is slightly more complicated. In the first place, all matter is largely space…"

In a room between the laboratory and the court, Marcus M. Drake paused by the door. Dr. Silverhead's conversation never interested him, but here was something new and strange in the doctor's manner. Drake turned to his two henchmen, who were working with broom and dustpan, sweeping up a broken bottle.

"I'd like to know," Drake snarled in an undertone, "which of you birds got him started drinking…Well, somebody must have done it. He never paid any attention to women before, but watch him go. You'd think she had him hypnotized into telling everything."

"Don't worry, Boss, nobody'll ever be able to understand him," said Mac. "What about it, are we gonna take him in on this proposition of pullin' stakes, or ain't we?"

"It's been my intention all along," said Drake, "to leave him high and dry when we move out."

"What I want to know is, how soon are we gonna load up and git moved?" Krug asked. "I figure we're a couple days too late already, if we expected to take Hamilton Craig along for protection—"

MAC nudged him remindfully that that matter shouldn't be brought up. Hadn't they taken enough browbeating from their boss already for letting their prisoner get away? That was the very bonehead who was going to make their moving job doubly difficult.

Instead of simply backing a truck up to the south side of the building, loading up their goods and driving off, they now had a few alert police to look out for.

In fact, there were evidences that a trap was about to close in around them. With a doubled police patrol on two sides, a new force of night watchmen building the tenanted sections of the building, and busy electricians mounting floodlights over the court, Marcus Drake's two henchmen were sure that a change of climate was urgently needed.

They had even heard rumors that some work was going to be done on the old well, since there was very likely an accumulation of debris in the bottom of it.

"They'll have a sad surprise when they find it's clean as a whistle," said Marcus Drake. "One bolt makes that metal bottom as solid as concrete."

"I'll take care of it right away." Mac dumped the broken bottle in a wastebasket.

"Not today," said Drake. "Don't get in a hurry. We'll get out before any big trouble falls due. And we may have another deposit to make."

"In the well? You got another customer?"

"There's a troublemaker or two still at large, by my figuring," said Drake. "Even if we know how to bluff Hamilton Craig out, there's still a stray or two that you lazy louts haven't accounted for. If they get foolish and pop up in our way we'll give 'em the courtyard exit."

The men gathered up some empty cardboard cartons and Drake dumped out the contents of a green steel toolbox that would be used to pack part of the money in. They made their way up the stairs past the carpenters and plasterers to the part of the building that was still their private domain.

Meantime, Linda Lee continued her lesson in the mysteries of atoms, for the doctor had an amazing lot to tell her, with all sorts of charts and machines to illustrate his principles.

Her ability to turn into a card, he explained, was one of his applications of these processes involving the nature of matter.

"When you become a card, the process is somewhat related to freezing. The activities of the electrons that compose your body are made to subside and you are condensed into a form that requires much less space. You return to normal when your atomic makeup is restored to its original space-filling organization."

"Gosh!" Linda Lee gasped. "Then lots of makeup is what Ah must need if Ah want to be nohmal. Is that the idea?"

She began powdering her nose, though this hardly seemed to be the response that Dr. Silverhead expected. He kept pointing to the big pyramid machine, describing the various actions that were brought about by a combination of light waves and vast electrical energy.

"If this new lens performs as I expect it to," he said, "no error will occur in the reintegrating of the billions of electronic impulses. The twin mechanisms above each chute will double those billions of impulses and two reintegration's of the original body of atoms will occur."

LINDA LEE was fairly gasping. "Ah nevah heahd of anything so amazing befo'. Now do Ah know all about it?"

"No one ever knows all about it without going through it," said the doctor. "Allow me to demonstrate the difference in the lenses—the old one that only disintegrates, and the new one I'm ready to try. Now for a subject—" he paused, and his glittering gaze returned from the top of the ladder to focus upon Linda Lee. "Can you climb a ladder?"

"Me? Does yo' subject have to be a puhson? Won't it work on a chair or a lamp or a book?"

"Of course. Everything disintegrates and reintegrates in the same way, whether it be alive, like my subject the other night, or dead, like—er—" Dr. Silverhead groped for a suitable example, "—well, if I remember correctly, this subject had on his person some sort of garden tool—yes, a pair of pruning shears. And they were disintegrated, too, of course, along with him and his clothes and any valuables he may have carried."

Linda Lee glanced at her watch. It was time for her to get back to work. She had promised to take Cornelia's shift.

Dr. Silverhead walked along with her.

"Or *was* it pruning shears? Why should he have carried pruning shears?"

The point was mildly disturbing to the scientist's mind, so unaccustomed to bothering with trifles. He led Linda Lee to the door above the basement stairs, and his glittering eyes combed the row of small tools hanging on the wall.

"No, I must be mistaken," he concluded. "But whatever he had, it has vanished for good, the same as my subject."

Linda Lee turned to stare blankly at the doctor.

"Gee, do you mean this puhson y'all have been talkin' about has sure 'nuf *vanished fo' good?*"

"In the interests of scientific advancement, you understand."

Linda Lee gulped and shook her head slowly. "Aftah all yo' big wo'ds Ah still hones'ly don' know what yo're up to. Y'all ain't violatin' any laws, ah' ya?"

For a moment Dr. Silverhead closed his eyes reflectively. "Sometimes I wonder. But no—my business manager takes care of everything. You will soon come back and let me demonstrate the lenses?"

"Ah—Ah guess so," said Linda Lee.

She hurried on her way, her ears ringing with big wonderful words. Electrons. Atoms. Electrical impulses. Disintegration—or was it disamputation? Dr. Silverhead was certainly the most amazing man she had ever met.

CHAPTER TWENTY-FOUR
Wedding Invitation

THE WEDDING OF HAMILTON CRAIG WILL TAKE PLACE THIS COMING SATURDAY AT TWELVE O'CLOCK NOON IN THE GARDEN. SIX CRAIGETTES ARE REQUESTED TO ATTEND, DRESSED AS BRIDESMAIDS. THEY WILL ASSEMBLE AT THE ARCADE EAST OF THE OLD WELL.
—H.C.

THAT was the new sign that the girls found on the reception room bulletin board one morning. Patsy read it through, ran upstairs uttering unladylike words, and came down with a handful of darts. She spent the forenoon throwing at the thing.

The other girls were slightly less demonstrative; they too were angered. After the rumors that had come through the keyhole on the night following the rescue of Hamilton Craig, they were more than ever sensitive about any mention of his romantic tendencies.

"What makes him think I care to be a bridesmaid—one of six?" asked Genevieve disdainfully.

"Have you looked up his ancestry, dear?" Cornelia asked mockingly. The thrust brought a giggle from Linda Lee. The snobbery of Genevieve was becoming vulnerable.

In fact, Genevieve and her ancestors had come in for a bit of ridicule on the previous evening. When she had come in after another evening out with Benjamin Dodge, the girls had listened at the head of the reception room stairs and had overheard her doing some very proud boasting about her forefathers.

Then she had asked Benjamin Dodge pointblank whether *he* could claim any great-great-grandfathers at Plymouth Rock.

"So that's your trouble, is it, Genevieve? Your ancestors came over on the Mayflower?" Benjamin Dodge had asked.

"They didn't," Genevieve replied, "but they should have. They missed the boat by ten minutes. So you see they were a part of the original band. Their proud spirit is in my blood."

And that was when Patsy, with her radio at the top of the stairs, had suddenly turned the volume up and the announcer shouted, "What your blood needs is Peabody's Purple Pills."

It amused Benjamin Dodge so much that Genevieve and everyone else could hear him laughing all the way down the street.

Now, at Cornelia's mention of ancestors, Genevieve made a cold shoulder gesture and walked off without a word. Bridesmaids—all six of them?

That wasn't the way the Craigettes had heard it through the keyhole. The night of Hamilton Craig's rescue, the talk in the office adjoining the reception room had lasted for an intense hour.

Four curious impressions had come to the girls out of what they had overheard.

The first and most dramatic: Hamilton Craig intended to marry very soon in order not to lose an inheritance, and he expected to marry one of his six Craigettes.

Second and most mystifying: The two voices—H.C.'s and Craig's—were so nearly identical that the girls, unable to see either man, were not absolutely sure that it was Craig who made this breath-taking statement. It could have been that other tall gentleman who had given his name as H.C. The two of them were talking things over so rapidly and with such a complete understanding that it was almost as if one man were discussing his own private plans aloud. Obviously there was the highest degree of cooperation between these two friends. And their voices were so nearly identical that the girls at the keyhole, unable to see either of them, kept gasping, "Now which one said *that?*"

"That was Craig…"

"No, it was H.C."

"*Ssssssh!* They'll hear you."

Third among their confused impressions was that whichever man intended to do the marrying, he was—and had—been in love. And his friend forced him to admit that he had never ceased to be interested in someone, in spite of his habitual attitude that women were poison. The girl of his choice probably wasn't aware of his long-enduring affection for her. He couldn't help that. He wasn't demonstrative, and he had been exceedingly busy "both at the studio and here." (At this point in the revelations the girls were sure it was Hamilton Craig.)

Then at last it came through like a bolt of lightning that these two men were undecided on one important matter: Which of them was to do the marrying in order to save the inheritance?

IT WAS understood that in any event there would be an equitable division of the money. The man who married would take two-thirds. There was no argument about that.

But each man preferred a smaller share of the fortune rather than the burden of marriage—until the talk came back to the matter of this mysterious former love. Gradually they revived their hopes that this object of their affections (her name wasn't specifically mentioned) might be persuaded to accept one of them.

"Which one of us do you think she could learn to love?" said one of the voices.

"Shall we flip for it?" asked the other.

"It's a gamble, at best."

"I'd rather not."

"Then there is a shade of difference between us—"

"As a result of these weeks of contrasted experiences—the real estate falling to you, the studio to me."

"Our plan to keep our natures identical was doomed from the start. Every new experience will alter us. We may as well accept that fact."

The discussion turned down the avenue of psychology, and the quartet of keyhole listeners were lost in the deep subject matter. Retreating to their rooms, they had so much to talk about that the night's sleep was ruined. Patsy was certain that the mysterious former love was one of the six Craigettes, and Linda Lee agreed with her. But none of the four would take a bow; in fact, the whole group declared that they wanted nothing to do with either of these women-hating hermits whose affections were outweighed by a pending fortune—hardboiled Patsy sounding off most violently.

Privately the four girls doubtless had their separate opinions, as the other two—Hetty and Grace—also would have had, had they been present.

But the bulletin board notice that confronted them this morning caused a new flare-up of that group spirit of rebellion.

They were all to be bridesmaids? That suited them just fine! They certainly weren't interested in Hamilton Craig—or in his mysterious cousin—as a possible husband.

But if they had been buying bridal veils they couldn't have gone to any greater pains to choose.

"Six Craigettes are requested to attend." But what if there were only four?

Craig answered that question by posting another bulletin. He offered a liberal reward to anyone who would locate any of the three missing employees—Hetty, Grace, and Archie. He penned a postscript at the bottom:

THE WEDDING REQUIRES THE PRESENCE OF SIX CRAIGETTES

The offer of the reward impressed Cornelia more than the others because it bore a dollar sign. But all four of the girls had actually offered all the information they could about the missing persons. Since the night H.C. had made his appearance there had been a handful of private detectives at work on the case.

Cornelia, as bankrupt for clues as the others, nevertheless mobilized her Craigette Protective Association. Verrazzano neglected his salesmanship and became overly helpful in his obsequious way. A trio of bond salesmen also answered her call. However, she was unable to get in touch with Whiskey Phil Parker.

"Ah cain't believe but what he'll turn up soonah o' latah," Linda Lee would say, though every time she repeated it her childlike face would cloud with doubt.

No one guessed what a fog Linda Lee was walking through. Sometimes she thought she could not bear the weight of all these mysterious happenings. She must confide in someone. But whom?

Certainly not in Craig. He was much too busy. His private detectives? They were much too important, too snappish with their sharp questions:

"When did you last see Hetty and Grace? Speak up! Were they with Archie Burnette? What were they wearing? Which way did they go? You didn't notice? Why didn't you?"

NO, THOSE men were too unfriendly to confide in. Besides, today they were again searching the buildings and grounds and reporting their bad news to Hamilton Craig. (It was rumored among the tenants that some of the eccentric old doctor's friends were hiding out to avoid eviction—but of course the tenants knew nothing about the disappearance of Archie and the two Craigettes.)

Linda Lee's need of a confidant brought her back to the white-haired doctor with the sharp little beard who looked so much like a Kentucky colonel and who seemed to enjoy talking with her in big words.

Linda Lee crossed the court and entered the laboratory. She found Dr. Silverhead at work in a large room that had once been an auditorium within the old hospital. He was checking through boxes and crates of scientific equipment. He dropped the work at once, however, as soon as he saw her.

"All broken or damaged," he said, with a sweep of his arm toward the auditorium. "But unquestionably I can salvage enough of value to outweigh any rent bill. It's very strange I should be overdue. I must have a talk with Drake. But it's true I have yet to realize anything monetarily on my inventions. The few persons I've benefited—such as

Hamilton Craig—have been simply experiments. And now you—"

"Ah came to ask you some questions," said Linda Lee. "The othah day you told me about a subject—"

"Stop right there," said the doctor. "You'll see it all for yourself. Can you climb a ladder? Ah—but you suggested we try a book or a lamp. Very good."

Following him up the steps Linda Lee found herself on the stage again, gazing up at the huge gleaming pyramid of black tubes. Dr. Silverhead pressed a switch and the sparks snapped. He crawled up to the top of the ladder and threw a book into the slide.

Within a few seconds two books appeared at the base of the pyramid, one coming forth from each of the projecting chutes.

The doctor shed his coat and tossed it in. Moments later two coats came out, identical to the last frayed thread in the buttonholes.

From another room Marcus M. Drake and his two henchmen looked in and saw the impossible. That freakish mass of machinery did make some sort of sense after all! *One of the doctor's experiments was actually working!* (Up to this moment Drake had taken all the scientific talk about the duplication of objects to be so much hogwash).

Before Drake's and Mac's and Krug's amazed eyes it was happening!

They saw the doctor drop a pocketbook in at the top; they saw two identical pocketbooks slide out through the two lower chutes.

"All right, men, wake up," Drake snapped at his cohorts. "Do I have to tell you what to do? We've no time to lose."

"I don't getcha, Boss," said Mac.

"The money boxes, you numbskull. Get them down here. You saw what happened to his pocketbook."

"You're gonna trust us, for once?"

"If that machine holds out there'll be plenty for all of us." Drake's growl turned into an evil laugh. "We can start a full grown state of inflation. Come on, I'll go with you..."

PRANCING around the old stage among the panels of dilapidated scenery, Dr. Silverhead was so well pleased with himself that he could hardly speak. He pointed jubilantly to the most conspicuous six-inch lens.

"It took only a microscopic change to make all the difference—the vast difference between reintegrating and failing to reintegrate. Would you like me to illustrate?"

"Ah guess so," said Linda Lee. She thought she had never seen the scientist's eyes so bright. She watched him as he swiftly changed the lenses. He placed the good one carefully on a stand, inserted another.

"Now you'll see how badly the old lens works. For several weeks I was uncertain of the source of my trouble. Nothing would reintegrate. I'll illustrate, if you'll just climb up the ladder, please."

Linda Lee felt a little stage fright as she ascended. But soon she was at the top. She combed her hair while awaiting further orders, as if she wanted to be well groomed for whatever experience this demonstration might involve.

"One moment, please. I've made a mistake," Dr. Silverhead said casually. He paused to consider. "This demonstration of the inadequacy of the faulty lens is entirely for your benefit. You should come back down and scrutinize the developments from this angle."

Linda Lee obediently crawled down the ladder and stationed herself in front of the pyramid.

"For a moment, I was being rather absentminded. It would have been a mistake to let you serve as the subject.

You'd have missed seeing what comes out—or rather, what doesn't come out. I'll be the subject myself."

He turned on the switch and climbed to the top of the ladder. Then he slid down into the pyramid, and Linda Lee observed the results.

Precisely as he had predicted, nothing came out. After several minutes of waiting she decided the demonstration must be over. It was certainly the strangest demonstration she ever hoped to see. It was funny that the doctor would leave without saying a word about turning the switch off. But he didn't reappear—anywhere—after that.

CHAPTER TWENTY-FIVE
Money, Money, Money

THERE wasn't much time to crow about it, but Marcus M. Drake knew he'd played into the good fortune of a lifetime. That was what came of keeping your nerve and not being scared out at the first signs of trouble. Detectives floating through the place were there? Well, they'd better watch their step. Marcus Drake had one very special piece of work to do before he and his cronies were through around here.

"Hold tight to those money boxes, boys," Drake growled, leading the way down to the stage. "Time's short and nobody's goin' to block our path now."

"It ain't quite dark, Boss," said Mac. "It ain't a good time to risk any gunplay."

"Nobody's goin' to block our path," Drake repeated, a feverish eagerness in his voice. "We've invested too many slit throats in this wad to let it slip. But don't worry, kid, there'll be no shooting unless the cops gang up on us. Hell, you think I've lost my touch? The well's still out there."

Drake lowered his voice to keep his enthusiasm under control. There was the towering pyramid of black tubes, still popping and crackling with streams of purple sparks. Where was the doctor?

"Is Silverhead up on the next floor? Scout around, Krug, and find out what's happened to him."

"I'll get him," said Krug.

"Hell, no. If he's busy don't bother him. As long as the damn thing's running—Krug, come back. Get up the ladder and pour it in."

"Can't he drop it in, box and all, Boss?" Mac suggested. "Or does he have to send the bills through loose? You saw the Doc's pocketbook go through."

"Don't quibble!" Drake roared. "Drop the box in. Throw it in. Kick it in. Hurry up about it. And the other box—"

"He's got 'em both, if he don't bust the damn ladder," said Mac.

Krug made it to the top safely. He struggled to shift the weight of the two cases to the top of the slide.

Mac's imagination was beginning to grasp the wonders of this machine. He followed Marcus Drake to the middle of the stage where the two lower chutes emerged from the base of the machine, apparently ready to pour wealth at their feet.

"All those thousands, Boss. Think of it. We'll double 'em—"

"Double!" Drake sneered. "Didn't you get past the first grade? We'll put them through a hundred times, and then another hundred. Man, we'll pile up a mountain of bills. All we can cart away in our ten-ton truck—"

Krug shouted down from the pinnacle. "Here they go!"

The two boxes swished down the slide. Purple sparks continued to flow over the black tubes of the pyramid. But nothing came out of the two lower chutes. Something was wrong.

Marcus Drake's suspicions were always high. Had Krug sidetracked the boxes? "Go up that ladder, Mac, and see what's wrong."

For three frantic minutes Drake bounced around the machine, up the ladder, back down to the pay-off chutes. His mad investigation unearthed one shiny bit of evidence. Here was a substitute.

It was worth a try. He knew well enough after all of Dr. Silverhead's profuse fussing, where that lens might belong.

His puffy fingers trembled, but he succeeded in making the exchange. It could be that the little operation would put the machine in order. He tossed a screwdriver up to Krug, who was still perched on the top of the ladder.

"Throw it in," Drake yelled. "Maybe it'll knock the money loose."

Krug tossed the screwdriver into the slide. It disappeared. Ten or twelve seconds later two identical screwdrivers came out of the lower chutes. Drake held them up for the other to see.

"Now we're on the right track. We've got to find something big enough to gouge that money loose. Get that chair, Mac."

The chair went down the slide. Drake counted to ten. Two chairs struck the stage floor with a single thump.

But where was the money? Drake paced the floor like a madman. His henchmen felt black trouble looming around them. They made repeated experiments with other objects. The objects came through in duplicate—but no money.

Marcus Drake's fury turned on Krug.

"Damn you, you threw it in. You go in and find it."

"What? Me? Listen, Boss—"

"You heard me. Dive in, Krug. Go in kicking. Knock that dough loose, damn it, or I'll paste you to the wall with lead!"

"You wouldn't—"

"Oh, wouldn't I?" Drake swung his gun upward with a gesture full of blind rage. Krug dived into the slide and went down kicking.

Two Krugs came sprawling out of the lower chutes. They got up in unison and stared at each other with identical amazement. Then their glares turned upon Marcus Drake. Their not too friendly appearance had a calming effect upon their boss.

But he was still the boss. "Come here, you men. Come here, Mac. Let's talk this over."

"Well, what did happen to the money?" Mac growled.

"Whatever happened," said Marcus Drake, with an inspiration that was more diplomacy than generosity, "we'll have to re-divide it. There are four of us now."

The two Krugs nudged each other.

"But we'd better face the bitter fact," said Marcus Drake. "The machine gave us a misdeal. The only thing to do is start over. How much money do you boys have on you? Get that cigar box, Krug...hell, I didn't mean both of you...all right, toss your bills in, men, and we'll get this business rolling."

"It'll take us a devil of a long time to work up a thousand—"

"I knew you never got to the third grade, Mac," Drake taunted. "Now the idea is this. Every time two boxes come down we'll dump all the bills into one and discard the other. After we get one box jammed full, we'll tack it shut and get into high gear. Everything'll come through full. We'll stack half the boxes that come down and throw the other half back to the top for seed. Who's good at pickin' cigar boxes out of the air? You Krugs? All right, hike up the ladder, one of you. And for heaven's sake, don't fall in. I'll go nuts if any more of you spring up."

One of the Krugs ascended the ladder. Drake drew a satisfied breath and started to light a cigarette. But his shoulders stiffened and he tossed the cigarette aside.

"Anything wrong, Boss?" Mac asked.

"Keep the works goin', Mac," Drake bit his words. "I just saw a face at the door. To your left, toward the stairs."

"Who was it?"

"Someone I haven't seen for days—but I figure he's the guy that nearly clogged our waterworks a couple of times. Keep things going, Mac. It's dark out now. I'm going to take a little walk in the garden."

CHAPTER TWENTY-SIX
Long-Lost Archie

THE person Marcus Drake had caught sight of had made his appearance on these premises about an hour earlier. Most of that hour had been spent in the bar on the west side of the block.

It had taken two police officers several hours of cruising through the streets before they discovered that their passenger—whose memory was nearly a blank—must be familiar with this part of the city.

They had parked just off Southwest Boulevard and had led their charge along the streets, watching his reactions toward the various doorways.

"Do you know this place, young man?"

"I—I don't remember."

"We'll take him inside," said the sergeant.

The bartender blinked in surprise to see two strange officers entering. Then, noticing the young man between them, he said, "Hey, you're Archie, ain't you?"

"Is that your name?" the sergeant asked.

"I don't remember—could be."

The bartender raised an eyebrow. He hoped Archie wasn't in trouble.

"He's had a bad bump," said one of the officers. "And he came pretty near drowning a half mile out from shore. But he can't remember anything. Outside of that he's in pretty good shape. Aren't you, Archie?"

"I'm feeling all right."

"Remember me?" the bartender asked. "No? Say, I've got a letter someone left for you. Is it okay, officer, if I give him a letter?"

"Sure, go ahead. Maybe it'll help bring his memory back."

The officers watched Archie's puzzled face as he studied the letter. They took the bartender aside and told him all about the case. They were following through because they believed this young man must know about a gang of criminals. Some of his unconscious mumblings a few hours after his rescue had sounded as if he knew plenty.

But that wasn't all they had to go on.

They had found him floundering in the sea a half mile out from the storm sewer—only an hour after they had found the body of a murdered man along that same shore. This all appeared to be a follow-up of other similar murders as yet unsolved.

"If he gets his memory back," said the sergeant, "he may tell us things. And I figure we're on the right track to bring him back here."

"Didn't he have any identification?"

"Too badly soaked to be readable. He mumbled something about losing a gun. All he had besides his clothes was a little leather book. Would you believe it—they found him holding a wad of something up out of the water. It was a calm sea, and when he'd turn on his back he'd pack this wad on his chest, like he thought he could keep it out the water. He might have swum all day if they hadn't found him. Had no idea where he was going. His only purpose was to keep his packet dry. Of course it got soaked all the same."

"What was it?"

"His coat all bound up around this little leather book—hey, Archie!"

Archie looked up listlessly. He had laid the letter aside, preferring to devote his attention to his sandwich.

"Show the man your book, Archie."

ARCHIE unpinned the safety pin in the oversize coat the first-aid station had furnished him. He snapped the little leather book cover open long enough to reveal the single shiny white card it contained. Then he pinned it back in his pocket and went on eating his sandwich.

"Funny thing was, that card didn't seem to be wet," said one of the officers. "Some unusual material."

"A secret message, maybe," the bartender suggested.

"Just a blank card. No invisible ink or anything. We've hounded him to tell us what it means to him, and he says it's *the only thing of any importance*. That's all you can get out of him. I'm sure he's forgotten why it's important. Or else he's got his wires crossed and it don't amount to anything—"

"But just try to take it away from him," the other officer added. "To change the subject, am I right in figuring that that big storm-sewer crosses under this hill?"

"Damned if I know," said the bartender.

The officers asked Archie for his letter, and he welcomed them to read it aloud.

"Dear Archie, Drake's next snip will be a pip. Haw, haw! Get it? Some gag. It only cost a quarter."

"But I don't get it," Archie commented.

"He was drunk when he wrote it," said the bartender. "He was always drunk."

The officer read on:

"By the way, Archie, that sock in the jaw knocked sense in me. Not much but a little. Been meaning to see your boss but always forgot what I wanted to tell him. It's about my niece, Grace. She's really one swell kid—I know. If your boss only knew it, she would be one angel believe me, and I think I'll get out and quit making trouble. Tell him for me, will you, Archie?

Yours,

P. Parker."

"That's a queer letter," said the sergeant. "Who's P. Parker? You don't remember anyone by that name? Or the niece? What's the name of your boss?"

Archie shook his head slowly. "I'm trying—give me time."

"Take it easy," said the sergeant. "Tell you what. You just start out and walk around—anywhere you feel like walking. We'll talk with you some more after while. Go ahead."

Archie Burnette strolled halfway around the block, drifted through the old hospital building into the court. He followed along under the arcade, entered an open door, and looked into the laboratory.

And thus it was that he saw the Drake gang working feverishly around the big scientific instrument.

ARCHIE frowned. This was all so very vague, yet not completely unfamiliar. That thickset man putting a monocle to his eye—hadn't Archie seen him before?

Now the man slipped into a rough jacket and came over to Archie. He began talking about his garden. He carried a pair of pruning shears.

He led the way to an old well. He was being very friendly, but Archie wished it weren't so dark out here. What had happened to his friends, the officers? Were they following?

At the gardener's suggestion Archie bent down to try to see the water. Instantly the friendly hand on his shoulder became a heavy pressure on the back of his neck. Instantly the pruning shears came up and snapped at his throat.

It was an exceedingly strange experience. Did the gardener mean it for a joke or was he trying to do Archie injury?

The darkness was suddenly banished. All over the court there was bright light. A battery of floodlights had come on.

The gardener was snarling, glaring at the ineffectual tool in his hands.

"Rubber blades!" he growled, "flinging the tool in the bushes. He grabbed Archie with both hands. But two of his friends were rushing out to him yelling at him to layoff and come out of the light. Then Archie knew he felt like fighting, and he fought.

He whirled out of the grip of those puffy, sweaty hands. He smashed out with his fists. He landed a hard right that sent a shudder through the gardener's frame.

Then the fists flew. Under the floodlights the streaks of shadows jumped and crossed. Suddenly Archie caught a terrific blow on the point of the chin. He was seeing colored lights—lights in the back of his head. He bounced against the stone railing of the well.

That blow left him terribly groggy—but in some strange way it made everything clearer. *That man was Marcus Drake, whose business was murder.*

CHAPTER TWENTY-SEVEN
Free for All

GUNS began to pop. Archie sat up and rubbed his swollen cheek and gave his head a few twists to make sure it was still attached. The fight had almost done him in. Like a revolt breaking out over a peaceful village, the fracas had suddenly spread to all corners of the interior court.

A few police officers had popped up from somewhere and gunplay was the order of the day. Drake's slippery band leaped for cover and moved back toward the laboratory doorway, returning shot for shot.

Once Archie saw two Krugs running in the same direction, and he thought he was seeing things.

Once he saw a beautiful girl hurrying in through a doorway ahead of the gangster retreat, and she looked so much like Hetty that he knew he was seeing things.

But his hand slapped against his side and suddenly he knew. He was up with a bound, racing across the garden. That recent fistfight with Drake had ripped his coat pocket off and torn the leather book open. So Hetty had come to life! And now she was in the path of fire!

Hetty wasn't the only girl mixed up in this miniature war. Archie caught a glimpse of a Craigette with red hair, her eyes full of fire and hands full of brickbats. He ducked. She let fly with a brick and her aim was good. It caught one Krug in mid-flight and brought him down, and a second later an officer was on him.

"Not bad, sister!" the officer shouted. "Tell it to Craig," the girl snapped, beating it for cover.

Archie couldn't have taken a straighter course for the laboratory if he had been a bullet. As a matter of fact, he had flying bullets to direct him most of the way. He heard his sergeant shout, "Get that girl out of there!"

That was exactly what he meant to do. But Mac and Drake were following her. Not only for protection from bullets. As Archie cut in ahead of them he realized there was something else—a camera. What it contained would send Drake to the electric chair for sure. It was like Drake to think he could still beat the game.

"Get rid of it, Hetty!" Archie shouted. "They're after *it*, not you! Throw it away!"

She heard, and as she ran she looked for some place where she could safely hide it. But now Archie overtook her in a dead-end passage—a room on the second floor level, whose floor terminated before stage ropes, a ladder and some scientific apparatus.

Drake and Krug were pounding up the stairs.

Hetty hesitated at the brink, completely out of breath. Her sharp eyes were tinged with fear for once. She looked at the stage, and knew that the ladder was the only chance—and that she wasn't equal to it. Not with the camera.

"Give it to me," Archie snapped. "Anything to get rid of it."

He took it from her hands, tossed it at the one spot where he thought it might fall safely out of sight—a smooth metal slide at the top of the huge black electrical instrument. Then he caught Hetty up in his arms, crossed onto the ladder, facing forward and leaning back to take full advantage of its angle.

Archie and Hetty were halfway down when they heard some very conclusive shots from the floor above.

"That ought to get him!" It was the voice of Archie's sergeant. It was accompanied by a low, guttural groan that was unmistakably Marcus M. Drake.

The shooting and shouting and running had now come to a stop. The voices that Archie could hear were those of policemen who were feeling pretty well satisfied that they had cleaned house; and occasionally the bated words of wounded or handcuffed prisoners. Everything seemed so quiet.

So quiet that Hetty looked up at Archie with a curious smile, which reminded him that he was still standing on the seventh rung of the ladder.

It wasn't a particularly safe place to stop and talk, for the low snapping of purple sparks continued close by.

"Look down there, Archie," said Hetty, pointing to the stage floor. "Isn't that my camera?"

"Which one?" said Archie. "I see two of them."

"It won't take long to tell which is mine," Hetty said. "Mine has some pretty valuable films in it—and something else a whole lot more valuable. Did you ever miss one of your cards, Archie?"

"You mean Grace?"

"I was afraid we'd lose her that night in the tunnel, so I slipped her into my camera. I meant to tell you. I do hope she's all right."

CHAPTER TWENTY-EIGHT
Saturday Noon

THE hour had arrived. A warm sun shone down upon the garden. Radio music from one of the mansion windows provided a spirited background for the excited talk of four Craigettes dressed in bridesmaids' gowns. They were sitting at a card table sipping cokes.

EVERYONE in a gay and happy mood? Well, not exactly. What with no wedding in sight, no decorations, no bride, and no groom, they were not professing any raptures of delight.

But the excitement of the recent days gave them more than enough to talk about.

Carlo Verrazzano hailed them from across the path, and approached with many a deep bow and profuse apology for breaking in upon so lovely a foursome. However, he had some news that he thought should be conveyed to Cornelia without delay.

"Eet ees like you say, Meess Cornelia. Every time I put one bottle of our most wonderful perfume into the machine, two bottles come out. When I put in two, four come out."

"That's the very idea," said Cornelia. "I'm going to get rights on that machine, and we'll organize a big manufacturing concern. Now don't start getting tired, Carlo."

"She calls him Carlo," Genevieve whispered.

"But what I must tell you," Verrazzano continued, "I find a seegar box weeth money. Maybe counterfeet, maybe not. I take beeg magnifying glass out of macheene to look at eet. Veree good money. So I put seegar box in next, why not?"

"Well?"

"It never yet come out. I think macheene must be very broke."

"What about that magnifying glass?" Cornelia snapped. "Did you put it back where you got it?"

"Ooooh! Such bad luck. It slip out of my hands, break all to pieces."

"Oh—oh!" Cornelia caught her breath, and for a moment the other Craigettes thought she was going to turn into a card. But the effects of the original transformation were beginning to wear off. "There goes my last financial empire. I'm glad I didn't throw away that bond salesman's telephone number." Cornelia made a sharp gesture with her index finger. "As for you, Verrazzano, march right back and pick up the pieces. And don't speak to me again till you've put them back together."

"She doesn't call him Carlo," Genevieve whispered.

Verrazzano marched.

The habits of transforming into cards were definitely passing, the girls agreed. And Linda Lee said she had known all along it would be that way. The doctor had told her lots of things.

What other inside information had she been holding out? Well, there was the doctor's strange disappearance. She believed he might be gone for good. Maybe he wanted to live in some more spiritual realm or something. Yes, she practically saw him go. Honestly, he was the most miraculous person. He could duplicate anything with that wonderful machine. He admitted having performed experimental favors for Hamilton Craig. And it wasn't his fault if Craig had had a burst of bad temper and had torn out all those pretty copper ornaments in the office doorway.

GENEVIEVE kept glancing at her watch.

"Getting nervous?" said Cornelia. "I've known all along that you were Craig's mysterious one-time love."

"But I'm not," Genevieve said. "Benjamin Dodge and I— uh—" she smiled and all at once her haughtiness was melting. "We have a date as soon as this is over."

"Oh? I thought you two had quarreled over ancestors."

"When I tell you the latest you'll really laugh," said Genevieve, coming down off her snobbish high horse. "I can take it. I'm through being stuck up over ancestors. Ben showed me the records."

"She still calls him Ben," said Patsy.

"He showed me that my ancestors and his ancestors both missed the Mayflower by ten minutes because my ancestors were too slow getting his ancestors' boots blacked."

"Not really?"

"And when I get to be Mrs. Benjamin Dodge," said Genevieve, "I'll never hear the last of that."

"Then who is Craig going to marry? If it's one of us—"

"Maybe me," said Patsy with a toss of her red head. "He was awful proud of me when I knocked out that gangster with a brick."

"Don't worry," said Cornelia. "He'd never trust you with the crockery."

"He'll never get the chance," said Patsy, her hopes giving way to a flash of anger. "You think I'd ever be sap enough to love, honor, and *obey* a guy who'd marry to save a fortune?"

"For my part," said Cornelia, "that would depend on the size of the fortune. What about you, Linda Lee? You've been so quiet there must be something on your mind."

"Ah don' think Ah've got a mind," Linda Lee said sadly. "An' if y'all think that Ah'm Craig's suppressed desiah, yo' wrong. Ah'm off to college as soon as Ah can get packed. An' when Ah leahn my lessons Ah'm goin' to fall in love with a professah—one that knows all the big wohds."

"What Craig needs," said Genevieve, "is a nice, steady, devoted girl who will worship him all her life. I'm thinking of Grace—"

"She and Hetty are lost," said Cornelia. "We'll never see either of them again."

The girls fell silent. The blithe radio music sounded a discordant note upon their gloom. In recent days their hopes for their missing companions had been choked by unspoken terrors.

"Wait a minute," said Patsy. "Didn't I see Hetty the other night when the shooting was on? Sure I did. But I was so excited I—"

"You've been having those dreams too," said Genevieve.

"Ah have big wondahful dreams," Linda Lee mused, "whenever Ah come back from bein' a cahd. The doctah wouldn't tell me why. But I wondah if it isn't yo' mind floatin' round waitin' fo' yo' brain to get regravitated."

"I dreamed I was hearing Grace and her Uncle Phil talking," said Genevieve. "It all happened so quick that Grace couldn't believe he was dying."

"Dying?" said Cornelia. "Why, I caught the same dream—just as I was returning from my card state."

"That's what Ah was sayin'," Linda Lee gasped. "Ah was listenin' in, an' Ah heard Whiskey Phil say—"

"That he was sorry for all the harm he had done Grace," Patsy interrupted. "But I don't believe in dreams."

"THESE dreams are different," said Genevieve. "It's like Linda Lee said—for a minute your mind is sort of free. But all four of us couldn't have had that dream at the same time. What we overheard must have hung in the air or something. I wonder—"

"Ah wish we could ask the doctah."

"I wish we could talk with Grace and Hetty," said Patsy.

After comparing each of their stories, Genevieve found that she had caught a fuller dream than the others had. And they listened spellbound as she brought back the clear details. There had been something heart-rending in Whiskey Phil's last words. He had glanced back over his wrecked life. He kept apologizing for the way he had embarrassed Grace once—a long time ago—*in the presence of Hamilton Craig*—and it was awful.

"But she never knew Craig before," said Cornelia.

"I only know what I dreamed," said Genevieve staunchly. She was perfectly convinced that Grace had been Hamilton Craig's one-time love. All of Grace's preoccupation with morals had developed as her defense against her Uncle Phil's grotesque exhibitions of sinfulness.

"But in his last whispers he was trying to set things right," said Genevieve. "He told Grace she must forget him and be happy and bring back her sense of humor."

"An' she said she would try," said Linda Lee. "Ah remembah now."

"And then—the strangest thing," Genevieve went on. *"Hetty's voice came into the conversation.* And *she* promised that she and all of us Craigettes would help Grace. And finally, when Grace told her Uncle Phil goodbye, she was happy in her resolve. There. What do you make of it?"

Cornelia shook her head. "All I make of it is that Grace and Hetty are both dead."

"Don't you believe it," came Hetty's voice from the mansion path. "Or am I just the new maid bringing you girls some more drinks?"

EVENTUALLY a minister made his appearance on the scene—and a very dubious appearance it was—a supreme demonstration of confusion and helplessness. For with him came two identical grooms, both named Hamilton Craig, who were escorting two identical brides named Grace. The minister for the life of him couldn't get it through his head that he was *sure* to marry the right Grace to the right Craig, even though he couldn't tell either couple from the other. Both Craig's kept bombarding the poor fellow with confusing instructions, and both Graces were laughing so hard that they never thought to question the rights and wrongs of this unprecedented situation.

Tenants crowded down to the arcade doorway to see what was happening, and the Craig's shouted to them to come on and get in on the wedding party.

"Just one big happy family," said Patsy to the other exasperated bridesmaids.

And before any state of order could be attained and the bridesmaids could be made to understand where the duplicates had come from and the gathering cameramen and curiosity seekers could be quieted, one bridesmaid had been led away to a quiet corner for a few private words with the one lone best man.

"We may as well get into the spirit of this event," said Archie Burnette as he took Hetty's hands, "because as soon as it's over I'm going to go get a license. But first I've got to know whether you're going to turn into a card every time I kiss you. It would be darned inconvenient."

Hetty laughed. "That happened a few times because I was so surprised. But now—well, the truth is, I'm afraid I almost expect it."

Archie believed in putting theories to a practical test. And not a hasty test either. He removed the camera that hung from her shoulder, took her in his arms and kissed her.

"There. So you're not going back into a book?"

"At a time like this?" Hetty breathed. "If I do you can pack me on ice for life."

THE END

TOO INTENSE FOR THE AVERAGE READER?

This short novel caused a bit of a flap when it was first published in Amazing Stories back in 1957. It was initially rejected by two other well-known science-fiction magazines, and both times for similar reasons: "this story is simply too hot to handle" and "too dangerous for our book." However, the then editor of Amazing, Paul W. Fairman, was brave enough to accept and publish it. Fairman also queried Amazing's readers, wanting to know if they thought the tale was appropriate or not. All these years later this fine short novel still stands tall as a taut science fiction thriller and one of veteran author Henry Beam Piper's very best efforts.

ABOUT H. BEAM PIPER:

American sci-fi writer H. Beam Piper was born on March 23rd, 1904. He not only had a professed love of science fiction but was also an avid gun collector and prided himself in being a largely self-educated man.

For over fifteen years he was an often-published and critically acclaimed author. His first published short story, "Time and Time Again", appeared in the April, 1947 issue of *Astounding Science Fiction*. Although he wrote primarily short stories, Piper's legacy also included a number of memorable novels, including "The Space Viking," "The Cosmic Computer," "Little Fuzzy," "Null-ABC," and "Lone Star Planet," the latter of which was released by Ace Books as "A Planet For Texans." A posthumous work, "First Cycle," was published by Ace in 1982.

Although it has never been clearly established as to why, H. Beam Piper took his own life in November of 1964 at the age of 60. Some sources site depression over financial problems, while others attribute it as a spiteful act to prevent his ex-wife from collecting on a life insurance policy, which was null and void in the event of suicide.

EDGE OF THE KNIFE

By
H. BEAM PIPER

ARMCHAIR FICTION
PO Box 4369, Medford, Oregon 97501-0168

EDGE OF THE KNIFE
By H. Beam Piper

Chalmers stopped talking abruptly, warned by the sudden attentiveness of the class in front of him. They were all staring; even Guellick, in the fourth row, was almost half awake. Then one of them, taking his silence as an invitation to questions found his voice.

"You say Khalid ib'n Hussein's been assassinated?" he asked incredulously. "When did that happen?" There was no past—no future—only a great chaotic NOW.

"In 1973, at Basra." There was a touch of impatience in his voice; surely they ought to know that much. "He was shot, while leaving the Parliament Building, by an Egyptian Arab named Mohammed Noureed, with an old U. S. Army M3 submachine-gun. Noureed killed two of Khalid's guards and wounded another before he was overpowered. He was lynched on the spot by the crowd; stoned to death. Ostensibly, he and his accomplices were religious fanatics; however, there can be no doubt whatever that the murder was inspired, at least indirectly, by the Eastern Axis."

The class stirred like a grain-field in the wind. Some looked at him in blank amazement; some were hastily averting faces red with poorly suppressed laughter. For a moment he was puzzled, and then realization hit him like a blow in the stomach-pit. He'd forgotten, again.

"I didn't see anything in the papers about it," one boy was saying.

"The newscast, last evening, said Khalid was in Ankara, talking to the President of Turkey," another offered.

"Professor Chalmers, would you tell us just what effect Khalid's death had upon the Islamic Caliphate and the Middle Eastern situation in general?" a third voice asked with exaggerated solemnity. That was Kendrick, the class humorist; the question was pure baiting.

"Well, Mr. Kendrick, I'm afraid it's a little too early to assess the full results of a thing like that, if they can ever be fully assessed. For instance, who, in 1911, could have predicted all the consequences of the pistol-shot at Sarajevo? Who, even today, can guess what the history of the world would have been had Zangarra not missed Franklin Roosevelt in 1932? There's always that if."

He went on talking safe generalities as he glanced covertly at his watch. Only five minutes to the end of the period; thank heaven he hadn't made that slip at the beginning of the class. "For instance, tomorrow, when we take up the events in India from the First World War to the end of British rule, we will be largely concerned with another victim of the assassin's bullet, Mohandas K. Gandhi. You may ask yourselves, then, by how much that bullet altered the history of the Indian sub-continent. A word of warning, however: The events we will be discussing will be either contemporary with or prior to what was discussed today. I hope that you're all keeping your notes properly dated. It's always easy to become confused in matters of chronology."

He wished, too late, that he hadn't said that. It pointed up the very thing he was trying to play down, and raised a general laugh.

As soon as the room was empty, he hastened to his desk, snatched pencil and notepad. This had been a bad one, the worst yet; he hadn't heard the end of it by any means. He couldn't waste thought on that now, though.

This was all new and important; it had welled up suddenly and without warning into his conscious mind, and he must get it down in notes before the "memory"—even mentally, he always put that word into quotes—was lost. He was still scribbling furiously when the instructor who would use the room for the next period entered, followed by a few of his students. Chalmers finished, crammed the notes into his pocket, and went out into the hall.

Most of his own Modern History IV class had left the building and were on their way across the campus for science classes. A few, however, were joining groups for other classes here in Prescott Hall, and in every group, they were the center of interest. Sometimes, when they saw him, they would fall silent until he had passed; sometimes they didn't, and he caught snatches of conversation.

"Oh, brother! Did Chalmers really blow his jets this time!" one voice was saying.

"Bet he won't be around next year."

Another quartet, with their heads together, were talking more seriously.

"Well, I'm not majoring in History, myself, but I think it's an outrage that some people's diplomas are going to depend on grades given by a lunatic!"

"Mine will, and I'm not going to stand for it. My old man's president of the Alumni Association, and…"

That was something he had not thought of, before. It gave him an ugly start. He was still thinking about it as he turned into the side hall to the History Department offices and entered the cubicle he shared with a colleague. The colleague, old Pottgeiter, Medieval History, was emerging in a rush; short, rotund, gray-bearded, his arms full of books and papers, oblivious, as usual, to anything that had happened since the Battle of Bosworth or the Fall of

Constantinople. Chalmers stepped quickly out of his way and entered behind him. Marjorie Fenner, the secretary they also shared, was tidying up the old man's desk.

"Good morning, Doctor Chalmers." She looked at him keenly for a moment. "They give you a bad time again in Modern Four?"

Good Lord, did he show it that plainly? In any case, it was no use trying to kid Marjorie. She'd hear the whole story before the end of the day.

"Gave myself a bad time."

Marjorie, still fussing with Pottgeiter's desk, was about to say something in reply. Instead, she exclaimed in exasperation.

"Ohhh! That man! He's forgotten his notes again!" She gathered some papers from Pottgeiter's desk, rushing across the room and out the door with them.

For a while, he sat motionless, the books and notes for General European History II untouched in front of him. This was going to raise hell. It hadn't been the first slip he'd made, either; that thought kept recurring to him. There had been the time when he had alluded to the colonies on Mars and Venus. There had been the time he'd mentioned the secession of Canada from the British Commonwealth, and the time he'd called the U. N. the Terran Federation. And the time he'd tried to get a copy of Franchard's *Rise and Decline of the System States*, which wouldn't be published until the Twenty-eighth Century, out of the college library. None of those had drawn much comment, beyond a few student jokes about the history professor who lived in the future instead of the past. Now, however, they'd all be remembered, raked up, exaggerated, and added to what had happened this morning.

He sighed and sat down at Marjorie's typewriter and began transcribing his notes. Assassination of Khalid ib'n Hussein, the pro-Western leader of the newly formed Islamic Caliphate; period of anarchy in the Middle East; interfactional power-struggles; Turkish intervention. He wondered how long that would last; Khalid's son, Tallal ib'n Khalid, was at school in England when his father was—would be—killed. He would return, and eventually take his father's place, in time to bring the Caliphate into the Terran Federation when the general war came. There were some notes on that already; the war would result from an attempt by the Indian Communists to seize East Pakistan. The trouble was that he so seldom "remembered" an exact date. His "memory" of the year of Khalid's assassination was an exception.

Nineteen seventy-three—why, that was this year. He looked at the calendar. October 16, 1973. At very most, the Arab statesman had two and a half months to live. Would there be any possible way in which he could give a credible warning? He doubted it. Even if there were, he questioned whether he should—for that matter, whether he *could*—interfere…

He always lunched at the Faculty Club; today was no time to call attention to himself by breaking an established routine. As he entered, trying to avoid either a furtive slink or a chip-on-shoulder swagger, the crowd in the lobby stopped talking abruptly, then began again on an obviously changed subject. The word had gotten around, apparently. Handley, the head of the Latin Department, greeted him with a distantly polite nod. Pompous old owl; regarded himself, for some reason, as a sort of unofficial Dean of the Faculty. Probably didn't want to be seen fraternizing with controversial characters. One of the younger men, with a thin face and a mop of unruly hair, advanced to meet him as he came in, as cordial as Handley was remote.

"Oh, hello, Ed!" he greeted, clapping a hand on Chalmers' shoulder. "I was hoping I'd run into you. Can you have dinner with us this evening?" He was sincere.

"Well, thanks, Leonard. I'd like to, but I have a lot of work. Could you give me a rain-check?"

"Oh, surely. My wife was wishing you'd come around, but I know how it is. Some other evening?"

"Yes, indeed." He guided Fitch toward the diningroom door and nodded toward a table. "This doesn't look too crowded; let's sit here."

After lunch, he stopped in at his office. Marjorie Fenner was there, taking dictation from Pottgeiter; she nodded to him as he entered, but she had no summons to the president's office.

The summons was waiting for him, the next morning, when he entered the office after Modern History IV, a few minutes past ten.

"Doctor Whitburn just phoned," Marjorie said. "He'd like to see you, as soon as you have a vacant period."

"Which means right away. I shan't keep him waiting."

She started to say something, swallowed it, and then asked if he needed anything typed up for General European II.

"No, I have everything ready." He pocketed the pipe he had filled on entering, and went out.

The president of Blanley College sat hunched forward at his desk; he had rounded shoulders and round, pudgy fists and a round, bald head. He seemed to be expecting his visitor to stand at attention in front of him. Chalmers got the pipe out of his pocket, sat down in the desk-side chair, and snapped his lighter.

"Good morning, Doctor Whitburn," he said very pleasantly.

Whitburn's scowl deepened. "I hope I don't have to tell you why I wanted to see you," he began.

"I have an idea." Chalmers puffed until the pipe was drawing satisfactorily. "It might help you get started if you did, though."

"I don't suppose, at that, that you realize the full effect of your performance, yesterday morning, in Modern History Four," Whitburn replied. "I don't suppose you know, for instance, that I had to intervene at the last moment and suppress an editorial in the *Black and Green*, derisively critical of you and your teaching methods, and, by implication, of the administration of this college. You didn't hear about that, did you? No, living as you do in the future, you wouldn't."

"If the students who edit the *Black and Green* are dissatisfied with anything here, I'd imagine they ought to say so," Chalmers commented. "Isn't that what they teach in the journalism classes, that the purpose of journalism is to speak for the dissatisfied? Why make exception?"

"I should think you'd be grateful to me for trying to keep your behavior from being made a subject of public ridicule among your students. Why, this editorial which I suppressed actually went so far as to question your sanity!"

"I should suppose it might have sounded a good deal like that, to them. Of course, I have been preoccupied, lately, with an imaginative projection of present trends into the future. I'll quite freely admit that I should have kept my extracurricular work separate from my class and lecture work, but..."

"That's no excuse, even if I were sure it was true! What you did, while engaged in the serious teaching of history, was to indulge in a farrago of nonsense, obvious as such to any child, and damage not only your own standing with your class but the standing of Blanley College as well. Doctor Chalmers, if this were the first incident of the kind it would be bad enough, but it isn't. You've done things like this before, and I've warned you before. I assumed, then, that you were merely showing the effects of overwork, and I offered you a vacation, which you refused to take. Well, this is the limit. I'm compelled to request your immediate resignation."

Chalmers laughed. "A moment ago, you accused me of living in the future. It seems you're living in the past. Evidently you haven't heard about the Higher Education Faculty Tenure Act of 1963, or such things as tenure-contracts. Well, for your information, I have one; you signed it yourself, in case you've forgotten. If you want my resignation, you'll have to show cause, in a court of law, why my contract should be voided, and I don't think a slip of the tongue is a reason for voiding a contract that any court would accept."

Whitburn's face reddened. "You don't, don't you? Well, maybe it isn't, but insanity is. It's a very good reason for voiding a contract voidable on grounds of unfitness or incapacity to teach."

He had been expecting, and mentally shrinking from, just that. Now that it was out, however, he felt relieved. He gave another short laugh.

"You're willing to go into open court, covered by reporters from papers you can't control as you do this student sheet here, and testify that for the past twelve years you've had an insane professor on your faculty?"

"You're... You're trying to blackmail me?" Whitburn demanded, half rising.

"It isn't blackmail to tell a man that a bomb he's going to throw will blow up in his hand." Chalmers glanced quickly at his watch. "Now, Doctor Whitburn, if you have nothing further to discuss, I have a class in a few minutes. If you'll excuse me…"

He rose. For a moment, he stood facing Whitburn; when the college president said nothing, he inclined his head politely and turned, going out.

Whitburn's secretary gave the impression of having seated herself hastily at her desk the second before he opened the door. She watched him, round-eyed, as he went out into the hall.

He reached his own office ten minutes before time for the next class. Marjorie was typing something for Pottgeiter; he merely nodded to her, and picked up the phone. The call would have to go through the school exchange, and he had a suspicion that Whitburn kept a check on outside calls. That might not hurt any, he thought, dialing a number.

"Attorney Weill's office," the girl who answered said.

"Edward Chalmers. Is Mr. Weill in?"

She'd find out. He was; he answered in a few seconds.

"Hello, Stanly; Ed Chalmers. I think I'm going to need a little help. I'm having some trouble with President Whitburn, here at the college. A matter involving the validity of my tenure-contract. I don't want to go into it over this line. Have you anything on for lunch?"

"No, I haven't. When and where?" the lawyer asked.

He thought for a moment. Nowhere too close the campus, but not too far away.

"How about the Continental, Fontainbleu Room? Say twelve-fifteen."

"That'll be all right. Be seeing you."

Marjorie looked at him curiously as he gathered up the things he needed for the next class.

Stanly Weill had a thin dark-eyed face. He was frowning as he set down his coffee-cup.

"Ed, you ought to know better than to try to kid your lawyer," he said. "You say Whitburn's trying to force you to resign. With your contract, he can't do that, not without good and sufficient cause, and under the Faculty Tenure Law, that means something just an inch short of murder in the first degree. Now, what's Whitburn got on you?"

Beat around the bush and try to build a background, or come out with it at once and fill in the details afterward? He debated mentally for a moment, then decided upon the latter course.

"Well, it happens that I have the ability to prehend future events. I can, by concentrating, bring into my mind the history of the world, at least in general outline, for the next five thousand years. Whitburn thinks I'm crazy, mainly because I get confused at times and forget that something I know about hasn't happened yet."

Weill snatched the cigarette from his mouth to keep from swallowing it. As it was, he choked on a mouthful of smoke and coughed violently, then sat back in the booth seat, staring speechlessly.

"It started a little over three years ago," Chalmers continued. "Just after New Year's, 1970. I was getting up a series of seminars for some of my postgraduate students on extrapolation of present social and political trends to the middle of the next century, and I began to find that I was getting some very fixed and definite ideas of what the world of 2050 to 2070 would be like. Completely unified world, abolition of all national states under a single world sovereignty, colonies on Mars and Venus, that sort of thing. Some of these ideas didn't seem quite logical; a number of them were complete reversals of present trends, and a lot seemed to depend on arbitrary and unpredictable factors. Mind, this was before the first rocket landed on the Moon, when the whole moon-rocket and lunar-base project was a triple-top secret. But I knew, in the spring of 1970, that the first unmanned rocket would be called the *Kilroy*, and that it would be launched some time in 1971. You remember, when the news was released, it was stated that the rocket hadn't been christened until the day before it was launched, when somebody remembered that old 'Kilroy-was-here' thing from the Second World War. Well, I knew about it over a year in advance."

Weill had been listening in silence. He had a naturally skeptical face; his present expression mightn't really mean that he didn't believe what he was hearing.

"How'd you get all this stuff? In dreams?"

Chalmers shook his head. "It just came to me. I'd be sitting reading, or eating dinner, or talking to one of my classes, and the first thing I'd know, something out of the future would come bubbling up in me. It just kept pushing up into my conscious mind. I wouldn't have an idea of something one minute, and the next it would just be part of my general historical knowledge; I'd know it as positively as I know that Columbus discovered America in 1492. The only difference is that I can usually remember where I've read something in past history, but my future history I know without knowing how I know it."

"Ah, that's the question!" Weill pounced. "You don't know how you know it. Look, Ed, we've both studied psychology, elementary psychology at least. Anybody who has to work with people, these days, has to know some psychology. What makes you sure that these prophetic impressions of yours aren't manufactured in your own subconscious mind?"

"That's what I thought, at first. I thought my subconscious was just building up this stuff to fill the gaps in what I'd produced from logical extrapolation. I've always been a stickler for detail," he added, parenthetically. "It would be natural for me to supply details for the future. But, as I said, a lot of this stuff is based on unpredictable and arbitrary factors that can't be inferred from anything in the present. That left me with the alternatives of delusion or precognition, and if I ever came near going crazy, it was before the *Kilroy* landed and the news was released. After that, I knew which it was."

"And yet, you can't explain how you can have real knowledge of a thing before it happens. Before it exists," Weill said.

"I really don't need to. I'm satisfied with knowing that I know. But if you want me to furnish a theory, let's say that all these things really do exist, in the past or in the future, and that the present is just a moving knife-edge that separates the two. You can't even indicate the present. By the time you make up your mind to say, 'Now!' and transmit the impulse to your vocal organs, and utter the word, the original present moment is part of the past. The knife-edge has gone over it. Most people think they know only the present; what they know is the past, which they have already experienced, or read about. The difference with me is that I can see what's on both sides of the knife-edge."

Weill put another cigarette in his mouth and bent his head to the flame of his lighter. For a moment, he sat motionless, his thin face rigid.

"What do you want me to do?" he asked. "I'm a lawyer, not a psychiatrist."

"I want a lawyer. This is a legal matter. Whitburn's talking about voiding my tenure contract. You helped draw it; I have a right to expect you to help defend it."

"Ed, have you been talking about this to anybody else?" Weill asked.

"You're the first person I've mentioned it to. It's not the sort of thing you'd bring up casually, in a conversation."

"Then how'd Whitburn get hold of it?"

"He didn't, not the way I've given it to you. But I made a couple of slips, now and then. I made a bad one yesterday morning."

He told Weill about it and about his session with the president of the college that morning. The lawyer nodded.

"That was a bad one, but you handled Whitburn the right way," Weill said. "What he's most afraid of is publicity, getting the college mixed up in anything controversial, and above all, the reactions of the trustees and people like that. If Dacre or anybody else makes any trouble, he'll do his best to cover for you. Not willingly, of course, but because he'll know that that's the only way he can cover for himself. I don't think you'll have any more trouble with him. If you can keep your own nose clean, that is. Can you do that?"

"I believe so. Yesterday I got careless. I'll not do that again."

"You'd better not." Weill hesitated for a moment. "I said I was a lawyer, not a psychiatrist. I'm going to give you some psychiatrist's advice, though. Forget this whole thing. You say you can bring these impressions into your conscious mind by concentrating?" He waited briefly;

Chalmers nodded, and he continued: "Well, stop it. Stop trying to harbor this stuff. It's dangerous, Ed. Stop playing around with it."

"You think I'm crazy, too?"

Weill shook his head impatiently. "I didn't say that. But I'll say, now, that you're losing your grip on reality. You are constructing a system of fantasies, and the first thing you know, they will become your reality, and the world around you will be unreal and illusory. And that's a state of mental incompetence that I can recognize, as a lawyer."

"How about the *Kilroy*?"

Weill looked at him intently. "Ed, are you sure you did have that experience?" he asked. "I'm not trying to imply that you're consciously lying to me about that. I am suggesting that you manufactured a memory of that incident in your subconscious mind, and are deluding yourself into thinking that you knew about it in advance. False memory is a fairly common thing, in cases like this. Even the little psychology I know, I've heard about that. There's been talk about rockets to the Moon for years. You included something about that in your future-history fantasy, and then, after the event, you convinced yourself that you'd known all about it, including the impromptu christening of the rocket, all along."

A hot retort rose to his lips; he swallowed it hastily. Instead, he nodded amicably.

"That's a point worth thinking of. But right now, what I want to know is, will you represent me in case Whitburn does take this to court and does try to void my contract?"

"Oh, yes; as you said, I have an obligation to defend the contracts I draw up. But you'll have to avoid giving him any further reason for trying to void it. Don't make any more of these slips. Watch what you say, in class or out of it. And above all, don't talk about this to anybody. Don't tell anybody that you can foresee the future, or even talk about future probabilities. Your business is with the past; stick to it."

The afternoon passed quietly enough. Word of his defiance of Whitburn had gotten around among the faculty—Whitburn might have his secretary scared witless in his office, but not gossipless outside it—though it hadn't seemed to have leaked down to the students yet. Handley, the Latin professor, managed to waylay him in a hallway, a hallway Handley didn't normally use.

"The tenure-contract system under which we hold our positions here is one of our most valuable safeguards," he said, after exchanging greetings. "It was only won after a struggle, in a time of public animosity toward all intellectuals, and even now, our professional position would be most insecure without it."

"Yes. I found that out today, if I hadn't known it when I took part in the struggle you speak of."

"It should not be jeopardized," Handley declared.

"You think I'm jeopardizing it?"

Handley frowned. He didn't like being pushed out of the safety of generalization into specific cases.

"Well, now that you make that point, yes. I do. If Doctor Whitburn tries to make an issue of...of what happened yesterday...and if the court decides against you, you can see the position all of us will be in."

"What do you think I should have done? Given him my resignation when he demanded it? We have our tenure-contracts, and the system was instituted to prevent just the sort of arbitrary action Whitburn tried to take with me today. If he wants to go to court, he'll find that out."

"And if he wins, he'll establish a precedent that will threaten the security of every college and university faculty member in the state. In any state where there's a tenure law."

Leonard Fitch, the psychologist, took an opposite attitude. As Chalmers was leaving the college at the end of the afternoon, Fitch cut across the campus to intercept him.

"I heard about the way you stood up to Whitburn this morning, Ed," he said. "Glad you did it. I only wish I'd done something like that three years ago... Think he's going to give you any real trouble?"

"I doubt it."

"Well, I'm on your side if he does. I won't be the only one, either."

"Well, thank you, Leonard. It always helps to know that. I don't think there'll be any more trouble, though."

He dined alone at his apartment, and sat over his coffee, outlining his work for the next day. When both were finished, he dallied indecisively, Weill's words echoing through his mind and raising doubts. It was possible that he had been manufacturing the whole thing in his subconscious mind. That was, at least, a more plausible theory than any he had constructed to explain an ability to produce real knowledge of the future. Of course, there was that business about the *Kilroy*. That had been too close on too many points to be dismissed as coincidence. Then, again, Weill's words came back to disquiet him. Had he really gotten that before the event, as he believed, or had he only imagined, later, that he had?

There was one way to settle that. He rose quickly and went to the filing-cabinet where he kept his future-history notes and began pulling out envelopes. There was nothing about the *Kilroy* in the Twentieth Century file, where it should be, although he examined each sheet of notes carefully. The possibility that his notes on that might have been filed out of place by mistake occurred to him; he looked in every other envelope. The notes, as far as they went, were all filed in order, and each one bore, beside the future date of occurrence, the date on which the knowledge—or must he call it delusion?—had come to him. But there was no note on the landing of the first unmanned rocket on Luna.

He put the notes away and went back to his desk, rummaging through the drawers, and finding nothing. He searched everywhere in the apartment where a sheet of paper could have been mislaid, taking all his books, one by one, from the shelves and leafing through them, even books he knew he had not touched for more than three years. In the end, he sat down again at his desk, defeated. The note on the *Kilroy* simply did not exist.

Of course, that didn't settle it, as finding the note would have. He remembered—or believed he remembered—having gotten that item of knowledge—or delusion—in 1970, shortly before the end of the school term. It hadn't been until after the fall opening of school that he had begun making notes. He could have had the knowledge of the robot rocket in his mind then, and neglected putting it on paper.

He undressed, put on his pajamas, poured himself a drink, and went to bed. Three hours later, still awake, he got up, and poured himself another, bigger, drink. Somehow, eventually, he fell asleep.

The next morning, he searched his desk and bookcase in the office at school. He had never kept a diary; now he was wishing that he had. That might have contained something that would be evidence, one way or the other. All day, he vacillated between conviction of the reality of his future knowledge and resolution to have no more to do with it. Once he decided to destroy all the notes he had made, and thought of making a special study of some facet of history, and writing another book, to occupy his mind.

After lunch, he found that more data on the period immediately before the Thirty Days' War was coming into his consciousness. He resolutely suppressed it, knowing as he did that it might never come to him again. That evening, too, he cooked dinner for himself at his apartment, and laid out his class-work for the next day. He'd better not stay in that evening; too much temptation to settle himself by the living-room fire with his pipe and his notepad and indulge in the vice he had determined to renounce. After a little debate, he decided upon a movie; he put on again the suit he had taken off on coming home, and went out.

The picture, a random choice among the three shows in the neighborhood, was about Seventeenth Century buccaneers; exciting action and a sound-track loud with shots and cutlass-clashing. He let himself be drawn into it completely, and, until it was finished, he was able to forget both the college and the history of the future. But, as he walked home, he was struck by the parallel between the buccaneers of the West Indies and the space-pirates in the days of the dissolution of the First Galactic Empire, in the Tenth Century of the Interstellar Era. He hadn't been too clear on that period, and he found new data rising in his mind; he hurried his steps, almost running upstairs to his room. It was long after midnight before he had finished the notes he had begun on his return home.

Well, that had been a mistake, but he wouldn't make it again. He determined again to destroy his notes, and began casting about for a subject which would occupy his mind to the exclusion of the future. Not the Spanish Conquistadores; that was too much like the early period of interstellar expansion. He thought for a time of the Sepoy Mutiny, and then rejected it—he could "remember" something much like that on one of the planets of the Beta Hydrae system, in the Fourth Century of the Atomic Era. There were so few things, in the history of the past, which did not have their counter-parts in the future. That evening, too, he stayed at home, preparing for his various classes for the rest of the week and making copious notes on what he would talk about to each. He needed more whiskey to get to sleep that night.

Whitburn gave him no more trouble, and if any of the trustees or influential alumni made any protest about what had happened in Modern History IV, he heard nothing about it. He managed to conduct his classes without further incidents, and spent his evenings trying, not always successfully, to avoid drifting into "memories" of the future...

He came into his office that morning tired and unrefreshed by the few hours' sleep he had gotten the night before, edgy from the strain, of trying to adjust his mind to the world of Blanley College in mid-April of 1973. Pottgeiter hadn't arrived yet, but Marjorie Fenner was waiting for him; a newspaper in her hand, almost bursting with excitement.

"Here; have you seen it, Doctor Chalmers?" she asked as he entered.

He shook his head. He ought to read the papers more, to keep track of the advancing knife-edge that divided what he might talk about from what he wasn't supposed to know, but each morning he seemed to have less and less time to get ready for work.

"Well, look! Look at that!"

She thrust the paper into his hands, still folded, the big, black headline where he could see it.

KHALID IB'N HUSSEIN ASSASSINATED

He glanced over the leading paragraphs. Leader of Islamic Caliphate shot to death in Basra...leaving Parliament Building for his palace outside the city...fanatic, identified as an Egyptian named Mohammed Noureed...old American submachine-gun...two guards killed and a third seriously wounded...seized by infuriated mob and stoned to death on the spot...

For a moment, he felt guilt, until he realized that nothing he could have done could have altered the event. The death of Khalid ib'n Hussein, and all the millions of other deaths that would follow it, were fixed in the matrix of the space-time continuum. Including, maybe, the death of an obscure professor of Modern History named Edward Chalmers.

"At least, this'll be the end of that silly flap about what happened a month ago in Modern Four. This is modern history, now; I can talk about it without a lot of fools yelling their heads off."

She was staring at him wide-eyed. No doubt horrified at his cold-blooded attitude toward what was really a shocking and senseless crime.

"Yes, of course; the man's dead. So's Julius Caesar, but we've gotten over being shocked at his murder."

He would have to talk about it in Modern History IV, he supposed; explain why Khalid's death was necessary to the policies of the Eastern Axis, and what the consequences would be. How it would hasten the complete dissolution of the old U. N., already weakened by the crisis over the Eastern demands for the demilitarization and internationalization of the United States Lunar Base, and necessitate the formation of the Terran Federation, and how it would lead, eventually, to the Thirty Days' War. No, he couldn't talk about that; that was on the wrong side of the knife-edge. Have to be careful about the knife-edge; too easy to cut himself on it.

Nobody in Modern History IV was seated when he entered the room; they were all crowded between the door and his desk. He stood blinking, wondering why they were giving him an ovation, and why Kendrick and Dacre were so abjectly apologetic. Great heavens, did it take the murder of the greatest Moslem since Saladin to convince people that he wasn't crazy?

Before the period was over, Whitburn's secretary entered with a note in the college president's hand and over his signature; requesting Chalmers to come to his office immediately and without delay. Just like that; expected him to walk right out of his class. He was protesting as he entered the president's office. Whitburn cut him off short.

"Doctor Chalmers,"—Whitburn had risen behind his desk as the door opened—"I certainly hope that you can realize that there was nothing but the most purely coincidental connection between the event featured in this morning's newspapers and your performance, a month ago, in Modern History Four," he began.

"I realize nothing of the sort. The death of Khalid ib'n Hussein is a fact of history, unalterably set in its proper place in time-sequence. It was a fact of history a month ago no less than today."

"So that's going to be your attitude; that your wild utterances of a month ago have now been vindicated as fulfilled prophesies? And I suppose you intend to exploit this—this coincidence—to the utmost. The involvement of Blanley College in a mess of sensational publicity means nothing to you, I presume."

"I haven't any idea what you're talking about."

"You mean to tell me that you didn't give this story to the local newspaper, the *Valley Times*?" Whitburn demanded.

"I did not. I haven't mentioned the subject to anybody connected with the *Times*, or anybody else, for that matter. Except my attorney, a month ago, when you were threatening to repudiate the contract you signed with me."

"I suppose I'm expected to take your word for that?"

"Yes, you are. Unless you care to call me a liar in so many words." He moved a step closer. Lloyd Whitburn outweighed him by fifty pounds, but most of the difference was fat. Whitburn must have realized that, too.

"No, no; if you say you haven't talked about it to the *Valley Times*, that's enough," he said hastily. "But somebody did. A reporter was here not twenty minutes ago; he refused to say who had given him the story, but he wanted to question me about it."

"What did you tell him?"

"I refused to make any statement whatever. I also called Colonel Tighlman, the owner of the paper, and asked him, very reasonably, to suppress the story. I thought that my own position and the importance of

Blanley College to this town entitled me to that much consideration." Whitburn's face became almost purple. "He...he laughed at me!"

"Newspaper people don't like to be told to kill stories. Not even by college presidents. That's only made things worse. Personally, I don't relish the prospect of having this publicized, any more than you do. I can assure you that I shall be most guarded if any of the *Times* reporters talk to me about it, and if I have time to get back to my class before the end of the period, I shall ask them, as a personal favor, not to discuss the matter outside."

Whitburn didn't take the hint. Instead, he paced back and forth, storming about the reporter, the newspaper owner, whoever had given the story to the paper, and finally Chalmers himself. He was livid with rage.

"You certainly can't imagine that when you made those remarks in class you actually possessed any knowledge of a thing that was still a month in the future," he spluttered. "Why, it's ridiculous! Utterly preposterous!"

"Unusual, I'll admit. But the fact remains that I did. I should, of course, have been more careful, and not confused future with past events. The students didn't understand..."

Whitburn half-turned, stopping short.

"My God, man! You *are* crazy!" he cried, horrified.

The period-bell was ringing as he left Whitburn's office; that meant that the twenty-three students were scattering over the campus, talking like mad. He shrugged. Keeping them quiet about a thing like this wouldn't have been possible in any case. When he entered his office, Stanly Weill was waiting for him. The lawyer drew him out into the hallway quickly.

"For God's sake, have you been talking to the papers?" he demanded. "After what I told you…"

"No, but somebody has." He told about the call to Whitburn's office, and the latter's behavior. Weill cursed the college president bitterly.

"Any time you want to get a story in the *Valley Times*, just order Frank Tighlman not to print it. Well, if you haven't talked, don't."

"Suppose somebody asks me?"

"A reporter, no comment. Anybody else, none of his damn business. And above all, don't let anybody finagle you into making any claims about knowing the future. I thought we had this under control; now that it's out in the open, what that fool Whitburn'll do is anybody's guess."

Leonard Fitch met him as he entered the Faculty Club, sizzling with excitement.

"Ed, this has done it!" he began, jubilantly. "This is one nobody can laugh off. It's direct proof of precognition, and because of the prominence of the event, everybody will hear about it. And it simply can't be dismissed as coincidence…"

"Whitburn's trying to do that."

"Whitburn's a fool if he is," another man said calmly. Turning, he saw that the speaker was Tom Smith, one of the math professors. "I figured the odds against that being chance. There are a lot of variables that might affect it one way or another, but ten to the fifteenth power is what I get for a sort of median figure."

"Did you give that story to the *Valley Times?*" he asked Fitch, suspicion rising and dragging anger up after it.

"Of course, I did," Fitch said. "I'll admit, I had to go behind your back and have some of my postgrads get statements from the boys in your history class, but you wouldn't talk about it yourself..."

Tom Smith was standing beside him. He was twenty years younger than Chalmers, he was an amateur boxer, and he had good reflexes. He caught Chalmers' arm as it was traveling back for an uppercut, and held it.

"Take it easy, Ed; you don't want to start a slugfest in here. This is the Faculty Club; remember?"

"I won't, Tom; it wouldn't prove anything if I did." He turned to Fitch. "I won't talk about sending your students to pump mine, but at least you could have told me before you gave that story out."

"I don't know what you're sore about," Fitch defended himself. "I believed in you when everybody else thought you were crazy, and if I hadn't collected signed and dated statements from your boys, there'd have been no substantiation. It happens that extrasensory perception means as much to me as history does to you. I've believed in it ever since I read about Rhine's work, when I was a kid. I worked in ESP for a long time. Then I had a chance to get a full professorship by coming here, and after I did, I found that I couldn't go on with it, because Whitburn's president here, and he's a stupid old bigot with an air-locked mind..."

"Yes." His anger died down as Fitch spoke. "I'm glad Tom stopped me from making an ass of myself. I can see your side of it." Maybe that was the curse of the professional intellectual, an ability to see everybody's side of everything. He thought for a moment. "What else did you do, beside hand this story to the *Valley Times?* I'd better hear all about it."

"I phoned the secretary of the American Institute of Psionics and Parapsychology, as soon as I saw this morning's paper. With the time-difference to the East Coast, I got him just as he reached his office. He advised me to give the thing the widest possible publicity; he thought that would advance the recognition and study of parapsychology. A case like this can't be ignored; it will demand serious study..."

"Well, you got your publicity, all right. I'm up to my neck in it."

There was an uproar outside. The doorman was saying, firmly:

"This is the Faculty Club, gentlemen; it's for members only. I don't care if you gentlemen are the press, you simply cannot come in here."

"We're all up to our necks in it," Smith said. "Leonard, I don't care what your motives were, you ought to have considered the effect on the rest of us first."

"This place will be a madhouse," Handley complained. "How we're going to get any of these students to keep their minds on their work..."

"I tell you, I don't know a confounded thing about it," Max Pottgeiter's voice rose petulantly at the door. "Are you trying to tell me that Professor Chalmers murdered some Arab? Ridiculous!"

He ate hastily and without enjoyment, and slipped through the kitchen and out the back door, cutting between two frat-houses and circling back to Prescott Hall. On the way, he paused momentarily and chuckled. The reporters, unable to storm the Faculty Club, had gone off in chase of other game and had cornered Lloyd Whitburn in front of Administration Center. They had a jeep with a sound-camera mounted on it, and were trying to get something for telecast. After gesticulating angrily, Whitburn broke away from them and dashed up the steps and into the building. A campus policeman stopped those who tried to follow.

His only afternoon class was American History III. He got through it somehow, though the class wasn't able to concentrate on the Reconstruction and the first election of Grover Cleveland. The halls were free of reporters, at least, and when it was over he hurried to the Library, going to the faculty reading-room in the rear, where he could smoke. There was nobody there but old Max Pottgeiter, smoking a cigar, his head bent over a book. The Medieval History professor looked up.

"Oh, hello, Chalmers. What the deuce is going on around here? Has everybody gone suddenly crazy?" he asked.

"Well, they seem to think I have," he said bitterly.

"They do? Stupid of them. What's all this about some Arab being shot? I didn't know there were any Arabs around here."

"Not here. At Basra." He told Pottgeiter what had happened.

"Well! I'm sorry to hear about that," the old man said. "I have a friend at Southern California, Bellingham, who knew Khalid very well. Was in the Middle East doing some research on the Byzantine Empire; Khalid was most helpful. Bellingham was quite impressed by him; said he was a wonderful man, and a fine scholar. Why would anybody want to kill a man like that?"

He explained in general terms. Pottgeiter nodded understandingly, assassination was a familiar feature of the medieval political landscape, too. Chalmers went on to elaborate. It was a relief to talk to somebody like Pottgeiter, who wasn't bothered by the present moment, but simply boycotted it. Eventually, the period-bell rang.

Pottgeiter looked at his watch, as from conditioned reflex, and then rose, saying that he had a class and excusing himself. He would have carried his cigar with him if Chalmers hadn't taken it away from him.

After Pottgeiter had gone Chalmers opened a book—he didn't notice what it was—and sat staring unseeing at the pages. So the moving knife-edge had come down on the end of Khalid ib'n Hussein's life; what were the events in the next segment of time, and the segments to follow? There would be bloody fighting all over the Middle East— with consternation, he remembered that he had been talking about that to Pottgeiter. The Turkish army would move in and try to restore order. There would be more trouble in northern Iran, the Indian Communists would invade Eastern Pakistan, and then the general war, so long dreaded, would come. How far in the future that was he could not "remember," nor how the nuclear-weapons stalemate that had so far prevented it would be broken. He knew that today, and for years before, nobody had dared start an all-out atomic war. Wars, now, were marginal skirmishes, like the one in Indonesia, or the steady underground conflict of subversion and sabotage that had come to be called the Subwar. And with the United States already in possession of a powerful Lunar base... He wished he could "remember" how events between the murder of Khalid and the Thirty Day's War had been spaced chronologically. Something of that had come to him, after the incident in Modern History IV, and he had driven it from his consciousness.

He didn't dare go home where the reporters would be sure to find him. He simply left the college, at the end of the school-day, and walked without conscious direction until darkness gathered. This morning, when he had seen the paper, he had said, and had actually believed, that the news of the murder in Basra would put an end to the trouble that had started a month ago in the Modern History class. It hadn't: the trouble, it seemed, was only beginning. And with the newspapers, and Whitburn, and Fitch, it could go on forever...

It was fully dark, now; his shadow fell ahead of him on the sidewalk, lengthening as he passed under and beyond a street-light, vanishing as he entered the stronger light of the one ahead. The windows of a cheap cafe reminded him that he was hungry, and he entered, going to a table and ordering something absently. There was a television screen over the combination bar and lunch-counter. Some kind of a comedy programme, at which an invisible studio-audience was laughing immoderately and without apparent cause. The roughly dressed customers along the counter didn't seem to see any more humor in it than he did. Then his food arrived on the table and he began to eat without really tasting it.

After a while, an alteration in the noises from the television penetrated his consciousness; a news-program had come on, and he raised his head. The screen showed a square in an Eastern city; the voice was saying:

"...Basra, where Khalid ib'n Hussein was assassinated early this morning—early afternoon, local time. This is the scene of the crime; the body of the murderer has been removed, but you can still see the stones with which he was pelted to death by the mob..."

A close-up of the square, still littered with torn-up paving-stones. A Caliphate army officer, displaying the weapon—it was an old M3, all right; Chalmers had used one of those things, himself, thirty years before, and he and his contemporaries had called it a "grease-gun." There were some recent pictures of Khalid, including one taken as he left the plane on his return from Ankara. He watched, absorbed; it was all exactly as he had "remembered" a month ago. It gratified him to see that his future "memories" were reliable in detail as well as generality.

"But the most amazing part of the story comes, not from Basra, but from Blanley College, in California," the commentator was saying, "where, it is revealed, the murder of Khalid was foretold, with uncanny accuracy, a month ago, by a history professor, Doctor Edward Chalmers..."

There was a picture of himself, in hat and overcoat, perfectly motionless, as though a brief moving glimpse were being prolonged. A glance at the background told him when and where it had been taken—a year and a half ago, at a convention at Harvard. These telecast people must save up every inch of old news-film they ever took. There were views of Blanley campus, and interviews with some of the Modern History IV boys, including Dacre and Kendrick. That was one of the things they'd been doing with that jeep-mounted sound-camera, this afternoon, then. The boys, some brashly, some embarrassedly, were substantiating the fact that he had, a month ago, described yesterday's event in detail. There was an interview with Leonard Fitch; the psychology professor was trying to explain the phenomenon of precognition in layman's terms, and making heavy going of it. And there was the mobbing of Whitburn in front of Administration Center. The college president was shouting denials of every question asked him, and as he turned and fled, the guffaws of the reporters were plainly audible.

An argument broke out along the counter.

"I don't believe it! How could anybody know all that about something before it happened?"

"Well, you heard that-there professor, what was his name. An' you heard all them boys…"

"Ah, college-boys; they'll do anything for a joke!"

"After refusing to be interviewed for telecast, the president of Blanley College finally consented to hold a press conference in his office, from which telecast cameras were barred. He denied the whole story categorically and stated that the boys in Professor Chalmers' class had concocted the whole thing as a hoax…"

"There! See what I told you!"

"…stating that Professor Chalmers is mentally unsound, and that he has been trying for years to oust him from his position on the Blanley faculty but has been unable to do so because of the provisions of the Faculty Tenure Act of 1963. Most of his remarks were in the nature of a polemic against this law, generally regarded as the college professors' bill of rights. It is to be stated here that other members of the Blanley faculty have unconditionally confirmed the fact that Doctor Chalmers did make the statements attributed to him a month ago, long before the death of Khalid ib'n Hussein…"

"Yah! How about *that*, now? How'ya gonna get around *that*?"

Beckoning the waitress, he paid his check and hurried out. Before he reached the door, he heard a voice, almost stuttering with excitement:

"Hey! Look! That's *him*!"

He began to run. He was two blocks from the cafe before he slowed to a walk again.

That night, he needed three shots of whiskey before he could get to sleep.

A delegation from the American Institute of Psionics and Parapsychology reached Blanley that morning, having taken a strato-plane from the East Coast. They had academic titles and degrees that even Lloyd Whitburn couldn't ignore. They talked with Leonard Fitch, and with the students from Modern History IV, and took statements. It wasn't until after General European History II that they caught up with Chalmers—an elderly man, with white hair and a ruddy face; a young man who looked like a heavy-weight boxer; a middle-aged man in tweeds who smoked a pipe and looked as though he ought to be more interested in grouse-shooting and flower-gardening than in clairvoyance and telepathy. The names of the first two meant nothing to Chalmers. They were important names in their own field, but it was not his field. The name of the third, who listened silently, he did not catch.

"You understand, gentlemen, that I'm having some difficulties with the college administration about this," he told them. "President Whitburn has even gone so far as to challenge my fitness to hold a position here."

"We've talked to him," the elderly man said. "It was not a very satisfactory discussion."

"President Whitburn's fitness to hold his own position could very easily be challenged," the young man added pugnaciously.

"Well, then, you see what my position is. I've consulted my attorney, Mr. Weill and he has advised me to make absolutely no statements of any sort about the matter."

"I understand," the eldest of the trio said. "But we're not the press, or anything like that. We can assure you that anything you tell us will be absolutely confidential." He looked inquiringly at the middle-aged man in tweeds, who nodded silently. "We can understand that the students in your modern history class are telling what is substantially the truth?"

"If you're thinking about that hoax statement of Whitburn's, that's a lot of idiotic drivel!" he said angrily. "I heard some of those boys on the telecast, last night; except for a few details in which they were confused, they all stated exactly what they heard me say in class a month ago."

"And we assume,"—again he glanced at the man in tweeds—"that you had no opportunity of knowing anything, at the time, about any actual plot against Khalid's life?"

The man in tweeds broke silence for the first time. "You can assume that. I don't even think this fellow Noureed knew anything about it, then."

"Well, we'd like to know, as nearly as you're able to tell us, just how you became the percipient of this knowledge of the future event of the death of Khalid ib'n Hussein," the young man began. "Was it through a dream, or a waking experience; did you visualize, or have an auditory impression, or did it simply come into your mind..."

"I'm sorry, gentlemen." He looked at his watch. "I have to be going somewhere, at once. In any case, I simply can't discuss the matter with you. I appreciate your position; I know how I'd feel if data of historical importance were being withheld from me. However, I trust that you will appreciate my position and spare me any further questioning."

That was all he allowed them to get out of him. They spent another few minutes being polite to one another; he invited them to lunch at the Faculty Club, and learned that they were lunching there as Fitch's guests. They went away trying to hide their disappointment.

The Psionics and Parapsychology people weren't the only delegation to reach Blanley that day. Enough of the trustees of the college lived in the San Francisco area to muster a quorum for a meeting the evening before; a committee, including James Dacre, the father of the boy in Modern History IV, was appointed to get the facts at first hand; they arrived about noon. They talked to some of the students, spent some time closeted with Whitburn, and were seen crossing the campus with the Parapsychology people. They didn't talk to Chalmers or Fitch. In the afternoon, Marjorie Fenner told Chalmers that his presence at a meeting, to be held that evening in Whitburn's office, was requested. The request, she said, had come from the trustees' committee, not from Whitburn; she also told him that Fitch would be there. Chalmers promptly phoned Stanly Weill.

"I'll be there along with you," the lawyer said. "If this trustees' committee is running it, they'll realize that this is a matter in which you're entitled to legal advice. I'll stop by your place and pick you up... You haven't been doing any talking, have you?"

He described the interview with the Psionics and Parapsychology people.

"That was all right... Was there a man with a mustache, in a brown tweed suit, with them?"

"Yes. I didn't catch his name..."

"It's Cutler. He's an Army major; Central Intelligence. His crowd's interested in whether you had any real advance information on this. He was in to see me, just a while ago. I have the impression he'd like to see this whole thing played down, so he'll be on our side, more or less and for the time being. I'll be around to your place about eight; in the meantime, don't do any more talking than you have to.

I hope we can get this straightened out, this evening. I'll have to go to Reno in a day or so to see a client there…"

The meeting in Whitburn's office had been set for eight-thirty; Weill saw to it that they arrived exactly on time. As they got out of his car at Administration Center and crossed to the steps, Chalmers had the feeling of going to a duel, accompanied by his second. The briefcase Weill was carrying may have given him the idea; it was flat and square-cornered, the size and shape of an old case of dueling pistols. He commented on it.

"Sound recorder," Weill said. "Loaded with a four-hour spool. No matter how long this thing lasts, I'll have a record of it, if I want to produce one in court."

Another party was arriving at the same time—the two Psionics and Parapsychology people and the Intelligence major, who seemed to have formed a working partnership. They all entered together, after a brief and guardedly polite exchange of greetings. There were voices raised in argument inside when they came to Whitburn's office. The college president was trying to keep Handley, Tom Smith, and Max Pottgeiter from entering his private room in the rear.

"It certainly is!" Handley was saying. "As faculty members, any controversy involving establishment of standards of fitness to teach under a tenure-contract concerns all of us, because any action taken in this case may establish a precedent which could affect the validity of our own contracts."

A big man with iron-gray hair appeared in the doorway of the private office behind Whitburn; James Dacre.

"These gentlemen have a substantial interest in this, Doctor Whitburn," he said. "If they're here as representatives of the college faculty, they have every right to be present."

Whitburn stood aside. Handley, Smith and Pottgeiter went through the door; the others followed. The other three members of the trustees' committee were already in the room. A few minutes later, Leonard Fitch arrived, also carrying a briefcase.

"Well, everybody seems to be here," Whitburn said, starting toward his chair behind the desk. "We might as well get this started."

"Yes. If you'll excuse me, Doctor." Dacre stepped in front of him and sat down at the desk. "I've been selected as chairman of this committee; I believe I'm presiding here. Start the recorder, somebody."

One of the other trustees went to the sound recorder beside the desk—a larger but probably not more efficient instrument than the one Weill had concealed in his briefcase—and flipped a switch. Then he and his companions dragged up chairs to flank Dacre's, and the rest seated themselves around the room. Old Pottgeiter took a seat next to Chalmers. Weill opened the case on his lap, reached inside, and closed it again.

"What are they trying to do, Ed?" Pottgeiter asked, in a loud whisper. "Throw you off the faculty? They can't do that, can they?"

"I don't know, Max. We'll see..."

"This isn't any formal hearing, and nobody's on trial here," Dacre was saying. "Any action will have to be taken by the board of trustees as a whole, at a regularly scheduled meeting. All we're trying to do is find out just what's happened here, and who, if anybody, is responsible..."

"Well, there's the man who's responsible!" Whitburn cried, pointing at Chalmers. "This whole thing grew out of his behavior in class a month ago, and I'll remind you that at the time I demanded his resignation!"

"I thought it was Doctor Fitch, here, who gave the story to the newspapers," one of the trustees, a man with red hair and a thin, eyeglassed face, objected.

"Doctor Fitch acted as any scientist should, in making public what he believed to be an important scientific discovery," the elder of the two Parapsychology men said. "He believed, and so do we, that he had discovered a significant instance of precognition—a case of real prior knowledge of a future event. He made a careful and systematic record of Professor Chalmers' statements, at least two weeks before the occurrence of the event to which they referred. It is entirely due to him that we know exactly what Professor Chalmers said and when he said it."

"Yes," his younger colleague added, "and in all my experience I've never heard anything more preposterous than this man Whitburn's attempt, yesterday, to deny the fact."

"Well, we're convinced that Doctor Chalmers did in fact say what he's alleged to have said, last month," Dacre began.

"Jim, I think we ought to get that established, for the record," another of the trustees put in. "Doctor Chalmers, is it true that you spoke, in the past tense, about the death of Khalid ib'n Hussein in one of your classes on the sixteenth of last month?"

Chalmers rose. "Yes, it is. And the next day, I was called into this room by Doctor Whitburn, who demanded my resignation from the faculty of this college because of it. Now, what I'd like to know is, why did Doctor Whitburn, in this same room, deny, yesterday, that I'd said anything of the sort, and accuse my students of concocting the story after the event as a hoax."

"One of them being my son," Dacre added. "I'd like to hear an answer to that, myself."

"So would I," Stanly Weill chimed in. "You know, my client has a good case against Doctor Whitburn for libel."

Chalmers looked around the room. Of the thirteen men around him, only Whitburn was an enemy. Some of the others were on his side, for one reason or another, but none of them were friends. Weill was his lawyer, obeying an obligation to a client which, at bottom, was an obligation to his own conscience. Handley was afraid of the possibility that a precedent might be established which would impair his own tenure-contract. Fitch, and the two men from the Institute of Psionics and Parapsychology were interested in him as a source of study-material. Dacre resented a slur upon his son; he and the others were interested in Blanley College as an institution, almost an abstraction. And the major in mufti was probably worrying about the consequences to military security of having a prophet at large. Then a hand gripped his shoulder, and a voice whispered in his ear:

"That's good, Ed; don't let them scare you!"

Old Max Pottgeiter, at least, was a friend.

"Doctor Whitburn, I'm asking you, and I expect an answer, why did you make such statements to the press, when you knew perfectly well that they were false?" Dacre demanded sharply.

"I knew nothing of the kind!" Whitburn blustered, showing, under the bluster, fear. "Yes, I demanded this man's resignation on the morning of October Seventeenth, the day after this incident occurred. It had come to my attention on several occasions that he was making wild and unreasonable assertions in class, and subjecting himself, and with himself the whole faculty of this college, to student ridicule. Why, there was actually an editorial about it written by the student editor of the campus paper, the *Black and Green.* I managed to prevent its publication..." He went on at some length about that. "If I might be permitted access to the drawers of my own desk," he added with elephantine sarcasm, "I could show you the editorial in question."

"You needn't bother; I have a carbon copy," Dacre told him. "We've all read it. If you did, at the time you suppressed it, you should have known what Doctor Chalmers said in class."

"I knew he'd talked a lot of poppycock about a man who was still living having been shot to death," Whitburn retorted. "And if something of the sort actually happened, what of it? Somebody's always taking a shot at one or another of these foreign dictators, and they can't miss all the time."

"You claim this was pure coincidence?" Fitch demanded. "A ten-point coincidence: Event of assassination, year of the event, place, circumstances, name of assassin, nationality of assassin, manner of killing, exact type of weapon used, guards killed and wounded along with Khalid, and fate of the assassin. If that's a simple and plausible coincidence, so's dealing ten royal flushes in succession in a poker game. Tom, you figured that out; what did you say the odds against it were?"

"Was all that actually stated by Doctor Chalmers a month ago?" one of the trustees asked, incredulously.

"It absolutely was. Look here, Mr. Dacre, gentlemen." Fitch came forward, unzipping his briefcase and pulling out papers. "Here are the signed statements of each of

Doctor Chalmers' twenty-three Modern History Four students, all made and dated before the assassination. You can refer to them as you please; they're in alphabetical order. And here." He unfolded a sheet of graph paper a yard long and almost as wide. "Here's a tabulated summary of the boys' statements. All agreed on the first point, the fact of the assassination. All agreed that the time was sometime this year. Twenty out of twenty-three agreed on Basra as the place. Why, seven of them even remembered the name of the assassin. That in itself is remarkable; Doctor Chalmers has an extremely intelligent and attentive class."

"They're attentive because they know he's always likely to do something crazy and make a circus out of himself," Whitburn interjected.

"And this isn't the only instance of Doctor Chalmers' precognitive ability," Fitch continued. "There have been a number of other cases…"

Chalmers jumped to his feet; Stanly Weill rose beside him, shoved the cased sound-recorder into his hands, and pushed him back into his seat.

"Gentlemen," the lawyer began, quietly but firmly and clearly. "This is all getting pretty badly out of hand. After all, this isn't an investigation of the actuality of precognition as a psychic phenomenon. What I'd like to hear, and what I haven't heard yet, is Doctor Whitburn's explanation of his contradictory statements that he knew about my client's alleged remarks on the evening after they were supposed to have been made and that, at the same time, the whole thing was a hoax concocted by his students."

"Are you implying that I'm a liar?" Whitburn bristled.

"I'm pointing out that you made a pair of contradictory statements, and I'm asking how you could do that knowingly and honestly," Weill retorted.

"What I meant," Whitburn began, with exaggerated slowness, as though speaking to an idiot, "was that yesterday, when those infernal reporters were badgering me, I really thought that some of Professor Chalmers' students had gotten together and given the *Valley Times* an exaggerated story about his insane maunderings a month ago. I hadn't imagined that a member of the faculty had been so lacking in loyalty to the college..."

"You couldn't imagine anybody with any more intellectual integrity than you have!" Fitch fairly yelled at him.

"You're as crazy as Chalmers!" Whitburn yelled back. He turned to the trustees. "You see the position I'm in, here, with this infernal Higher Education Faculty Tenure Act? I have a madman on my faculty, and can I get rid of him? No! I demand his resignation, and he laughs at me and goes running for his lawyer! And he is a madman! Nobody but a madman would talk the way he does. You think this Khalid ib'n Hussein business is the only time he's done anything like this? Why, I have a list of a dozen occasions when he's done something just as bad, only he didn't have a lucky coincidence to back him up. Trying to get books that don't exist out of the library, and then insisting that they're standard textbooks. Talking about the revolt of the colonies on Mars and Venus. Talking about something he calls the Terran Federation, some kind of a world empire. Or something he calls Operation Triple Cross that saved the country during some fantastic war he imagined..."

"*What did you say?*"

The question cracked out like a string of pistol shots. Everybody turned. The quiet man in the brown tweed suit had spoken; now he looked as though he were very much regretting it.

"Is there such a thing as Operation Triple Cross?" Fitch was asking.

"No, no. I never heard anything about that; that wasn't what I meant. It was this Terran Federation thing," the major said, a trifle too quickly and too smoothly. He turned to Chalmers. "You never did any work for PSPB; did you ever talk to anybody who did?" he asked.

"I don't even know what the letters mean," Chalmers replied.

"Politico-Strategic Planning Board. It's all pretty hush-hush, but this term Terran Federation is a tentative name for a proposed organization to take the place of the U. N. if that organization breaks up. It's nothing particularly important, and it only exists on paper."

It won't exist only on paper very long, Chalmers thought. He was wondering what Operation Triple Cross was; he had some notes on it, but he had forgotten what they were.

"Maybe he did pick that up from somebody who'd talked indiscreetly," Whitburn conceded. "But the rest of this tommyrot! Why, he was talking about how the city of Reno had been destroyed by an explosion and fire, literally wiped off the map. There's an example for you!"

He'd forgotten about that, too. It had been a relatively minor incident in the secret struggle of the Subwar; now he remembered having made a note about it. He was sure that it followed closely after the assassination of Khalid ib'n Hussein. He turned quickly to Weill.

"Didn't you say you had to go to Reno in a day or so?" he asked.

Weill hushed him urgently, pointing with his free hand to the recorder. The exchange prevented him from noticing that Max Pottgeiter had risen, until the old man was speaking.

"Are you trying to tell these people that Professor Chalmers is crazy?" he was demanding. "Why, he has one of the best minds on the campus. I was talking to him only yesterday, in the back room at the Library. You know," he went on apologetically, "my subject is Medieval History; I don't pay much attention to what's going on in the contemporary world, and I didn't understand, really, what all this excitement was about. But he explained the whole thing to me, and did it in terms that I could grasp, drawing some excellent parallels with the Byzantine Empire and the Crusades. All about the revolt at Damascus, and the sack of Beirut, and the war between Jordan and Saudi Arabia, and how the Turkish army intervened, and the invasion of Pakistan..."

"When did all this happen?" one of the trustees demanded.

Pottgeiter started to explain; Chalmers realized, sickly, how much of his future history he had poured into the trusting ear of the old medievalist, the day before.

"Good Lord, man; don't you read the papers at all?" another of the trustees asked.

"No! And I don't read inside-dope magazines, or science fiction. I read carefully substantiated facts. And I know when I'm talking to a sane and reasonable man. It isn't a common experience, around here."

Dacre passed a hand over his face. "Doctor Whitburn," he said, "I must admit that I came to this meeting strongly prejudiced against you, and I'll further admit that your own behavior here has done very little to dispel that prejudice. But I'm beginning to get some idea of what you have to contend with, here at Blanley, and I find that I must make a lot of allowances. I had no idea... Simply no idea at all."

"Look, you're getting a completely distorted picture of this, Mr. Dacre," Fitch broke in. "It's precisely as I believed; Doctor Chalmers is an unusually gifted precognitive percipient. You've seen, gentlemen, how his complicated chain of precognitions about the death of Khalid has been proven veridical; I'd stake my life that every one of these precognitions will be similarly verified. And I'll stake my professional reputation that the man is perfectly sane. Of course, abnormal psychology and psychopathology aren't my subjects, but..."

"They're not my subjects, either," Whitburn retorted, "but I know a lunatic by his ravings."

"Doctor Fitch is taking an entirely proper attitude," Pottgeiter said, "in pointing out that abnormal psychology is a specialized branch, outside his own field. I wouldn't dream, myself, of trying to offer a decisive opinion on some point of Roman, or Babylonian, history. Well, if the question of Doctor Chalmers' sanity is at issue here, let's consult somebody who specializes in insanity. I don't believe that anybody here is qualified even to express an opinion on that subject, Doctor Whitburn least of all."

Whitburn turned on him angrily. "Oh, shut up, you doddering old fool!" he shouted. "Look; there's another of them!" he told the trustees. "Another deadhead on the faculty that this Tenure Law keeps me from getting rid of. He's as bad as Chalmers, himself. You just heard that string of nonsense he was spouting. Why, his courses have been noted among the students for years as snap courses in which nobody ever has to do any work…"

Chalmers was on his feet again, thoroughly angry. Abuse of himself he could take; talking that way about gentle, learned, old Pottgeiter was something else.

"I think Doctor Pottgeiter's said the most reasonable thing I've heard since I came in here," he declared. "If my sanity is to be questioned, I insist that it be questioned by somebody qualified to do so."

Weill set his recorder on the floor and jumped up beside him, trying to haul him back into his seat.

"For God's sake, man! Sit down and shut up!" he hissed.

Chalmers shook off his hand. "No, I won't shut up! This is the only way to settle this, once and for all. And when my sanity's been vindicated, I'm going to sue this fellow…"

Whitburn started to make some retort, then stopped short. After a moment, he smiled nastily.

"Do I understand, Doctor Chalmers, that you would be willing to submit to psychiatric examination?" he asked.

"Don't agree; you're putting your foot in a trap," Weill told him urgently.

"Of course, I agree, as long as the examination is conducted by a properly qualified psychiatrist."

"How about Doctor Hauserman at Northern State Mental Hospital?" Whitburn asked quickly. "Would you agree to an examination by him?"

"Excellent!" Fitch exclaimed. "One of the best men in the field. I'd accept his opinion unreservedly."

Weill started to object again; Chalmers cut him off. "Doctor Hauserman will be quite satisfactory to me. The only question is, would he be available?"

"I think he would," Dacre said, glancing at his watch. "I wonder if he could be reached now." He got to his feet. "Telephone in your outer office, Doctor Whitburn? Fine. If you gentlemen will excuse me…"

It was a good fifteen minutes before he returned, smiling.

"Well, gentlemen, it's all arranged," he said. "Doctor Hauserman is quite willing to examine Doctor Chalmers— with the latter's consent, of course."

"He'll have it. In writing, if he wishes."

"Yes, I assured him on that point. He'll be here about noon tomorrow—it's a hundred and fifty miles from the hospital, but the doctor flies his own plane—and the examination can start at two in the afternoon. He seems familiar with the facilities of the psychology department, here; I assured him that they were at his disposal. Will that be satisfactory to you, Doctor Chalmers?"

"I have a class at that time, but one of the instructors can take it over—if holding classes will be possible around here tomorrow," he said. "Now, if you gentlemen will pardon me, I think I'll go home and get some sleep."

Weill came up to the apartment with him. He mixed a couple of drinks and they went into the living room with them.

"Just in case you don't know what you've gotten yourself into," Weill said, "this Hauserman isn't any ordinary couch-pilot; he's the state psychiatrist. If he gets the idea you aren't sane, he can commit you to a hospital, and I'll bet that's exactly what Whitburn had in mind when he suggested him. And I don't trust this man Dacre. I thought he was on our side, at the start, but that was before your friends got into the act." He frowned into his drink. "And I don't like the way that Intelligence major was acting, toward the last. If he thinks you know something you are not supposed to, a mental hospital may be his idea of a good place to put you away."

"You don't think this man Hauserman would allow himself to be influenced...? No. You just don't think I'm sane. Do you?"

"I know what Hauserman'll think. He'll think this future history business is a classical case of systematized schizoid delusion. I wish I'd never gotten into this case. I wish I'd never even heard of you! And another thing; in case you get past Hauserman all right, you can forget about that damage-suit bluff of mine. You would not stand a chance with it in court."

"In spite of what happened to Khalid?"

"After tomorrow, I won't stay in the same room with anybody who even mentions that name to me. Well, win or lose, it'll be over tomorrow and then I can leave here."

"Did you tell me you were going to Reno?" Chalmers asked. "Don't do it. You remember Whitburn mentioning how I spoke about an explosion there? It happened just a couple of days after the murder of Khalid. There was— will be—a trainload of high explosives in the railroad yard; it'll be the biggest non-nuclear explosion since the *Mont Blanc* blew up in Halifax harbor in World War One..."

Weill threw his drink into the fire; he must have avoided throwing the glass in with it by a last-second exercise of self-control.

"Well," he said, after a brief struggle to master himself. "One thing about the legal profession; you do hear the damnedest things! Good night, Professor. And try— please try, for the sake of your poor harried lawyer—to keep your mouth shut about things like that, at least till after you get through with Hauserman. And when you're talking to him, don't, don't, for heaven's sake, *don't,* volunteer anything!"

THE room was a pleasant, warmly-colored, place. There was a desk, much like the ones in the classrooms, and six or seven wicker armchairs. A lot of apparatus had been pushed back along the walls; the dust-covers were gay cretonne. There was a couch, with more apparatus, similarly covered, beside it. Hauserman was seated at the desk when Chalmers entered.

He rose, and they shook hands. A man of about his own age, smooth-faced, partially bald. Chalmers tried to guess something of the man's nature from his face, but could read nothing. A face well trained to keep its owner's secrets.

"Something to smoke, Professor," he began, offering his cigarette case.

"My pipe, if you don't mind." He got it out and filled it.

"Any of those chairs," Hauserman said, gesturing toward them.

They were all arranged to face the desk. He sat down, lighting his pipe. Hauserman nodded approvingly; he was behaving calmly, and didn't need being put at ease. They talked at random—at least, Hauserman tried to make it seem so—for some time about his work, his book about the French Revolution, current events. He picked his way carefully through the conversation, alert for traps which the psychiatrist might be laying for him. Finally, Hauserman said:

"Would you mind telling me just why you felt it advisable to request a psychiatric examination, Professor?"

"I didn't request it. But when the suggestion was made, by one of my friends, in reply to some aspersions of my sanity, I agreed to it."

"Good distinction. And why was your sanity questioned? I won't deny that I had heard of this affair, here, before Mr. Dacre called me, last evening, but I'd like to hear your version of it."

He went into that, from the original incident in Modern History IV, choosing every word carefully, trying to concentrate on making a good impression upon Hauserman, and at the same time finding that more "memories" of the future were beginning to seep past the barrier of his consciousness. He tried to dam them back; when he could not, he spoke with greater and greater care lest they leak into his speech.

"I can't recall the exact manner in which I blundered into it. The fact that I did make such a blunder was because I was talking extemporaneously and had wandered ahead of my text. I was trying to show the results of the collapse of the Ottoman Empire after the First World War, and the partition of the Middle East into a loose collection of Arab states, and the passing of British and other European spheres of influence following the Second. You know, when you consider it, the Islamic Caliphate was inevitable; the surprising thing is that it was created by a man like Khalid…"

He was talking to gain time, and he suspected that Hauserman knew it. The "memories" were coming into his mind more and more strongly; it was impossible to suppress them. The period of anarchy following Khalid's death would be much briefer, and much more violent, than he had previously thought. Tallal ib'n Khalid would be flying from England even now; perhaps he had already left the plane to take refuge among the black tents of his father's Bedouins. The revolt at Damascus would break out before the end of the month; before the end of the year, the whole of Syria and Lebanon would be in bloody chaos, and the Turkish army would be on the march.

"Yes. And you allowed yourself to be carried a little beyond the present moment, into the future, without realizing it? Is that it?"

"Something like that," he replied, wide awake to the trap Hauserman had set, and fearful that it might be a blind, to disguise the real trap. "History follows certain patterns. I'm not a Toynbean, by any manner of means, but any historian can see that certain forces generally tend to produce similar effects. For instance, space travel is now a fact; our government has at present a military base on Luna. Within our lifetimes—certainly within the lifetimes of my students—there will be explorations and attempts at colonization on Mars and Venus. You believe that, Doctor?"

"Oh, unreservedly. I'm not supposed to talk about it, but I did some work on the Philadelphia Project, myself. I'd say that every major problem of interplanetary flight had been solved before the first robot rocket was landed on Luna."

"Yes. And when Mars and Venus are colonized, there will be the same historic situations, at least in general shape, as arose when the European powers were colonizing the New World, or, for that matter, when the Greek city-states were throwing out colonies across the Aegean. That's the sort of thing we call projecting the past into the future through the present."

Hauserman nodded. "But how about the details? Things like the assassination of a specific personage. How can you extrapolate to a thing like that?"

"Well..." More "memories" were coming to the surface; he tried to crowd them back. "I do my projecting in what you might call fictionalized form; try to fill in the details from imagination. In the case of Khalid, I was trying to imagine what would happen if his influence were suddenly removed from Near Eastern and Middle Eastern, affairs. I suppose I constructed an imaginary scene of his assassination..."

He went on at length. Mohammed and Noureed were common enough names. The Middle East was full of old U. S. weapons. Stoning was the traditional method of execution; it diffused responsibility so that no individual could be singled out for blood-feud vengeance.

"You have no idea how disturbed I was when the whole thing happened, exactly as I had described it," he continued. "And worst of all, to me, was this Intelligence officer showing up; I thought I was really in for it!"

"Then you've never really believed that you had real knowledge of the future?"

"I'm beginning to, since I've been talking to these Psionics and Parapsychology people," he laughed. It sounded, he hoped, like a natural and unaffected laugh. "They seem to be convinced that I have."

There would be an Eastern-inspired uprising in Azerbaijan by the middle of the next year; before autumn, the Indian Communists would make their fatal attempt to seize East Pakistan. The Thirty Days' War would be the immediate result. By that time, the Lunar Base would be completed and ready; the enemy missiles would be aimed primarily at the rocketports from which it was supplied.

Delivered without warning, it should have succeeded—except that every rocketport had its secret duplicate and triplicate. That was Operation Triple Cross; no wonder Major Cutler had been so startled at the words, last evening. The enemy would be utterly overwhelmed under the rain of missiles from across space, but until the moon-rockets began to fall, the United States would suffer grievously.

"Honestly, though, I feel sorry for my friend Fitch," he added. "He's going to be frightfully let down when some more of my alleged prophecies misfire on him. But I really haven't been deliberately deceiving him."

And Blanley College was at the center of one of the areas which would receive the worst of the thermonuclear hell to come. And it would be a little under a year...

"And that's all there is to it!" Hauserman exclaimed, annoyance in his voice. "I'm amazed that this man Whitburn allowed a thing like this to assume the proportions it did. I must say that I seem to have gotten the story about this business in a very garbled form indeed." He laughed shortly. "I came here convinced that you were mentally unbalanced. I hope you won't take that the wrong way, Professor," he hastened to add. "In my profession, anything can be expected. A good psychiatrist can never afford to forget how sharp and fine is the knife-edge."

"The knife-edge!" The words startled him. He had been thinking, at that moment, of the knife-edge, slicing moment after moment relentlessly away from the future, into the past, at each slice coming closer and closer to the moment when the missiles of the Eastern Axis would fall. "I didn't know they still resorted to surgery, in mental cases," he added, trying to cover his break.

"Oh, no; all that sort of thing is as irrevocably discarded as the whips and shackles of Bedlam. I meant another kind of knife-edge; the thin, almost invisible, line which separates sanity from non-sanity. From madness, to use a deplorable lay expression." Hauserman lit another cigarette. "Most minds are a lot closer to it than their owners suspect, too. In fact, Professor, I was so convinced that yours had passed over it that I brought with me a commitment form, made out all but my signature, for you." He took it from his pocket and laid it on the desk. "The modern equivalent of the *lettre-de-cachet*, I suppose the author of a book on the French Revolution would call it. I was all ready to certify you as mentally unsound, and commit you to Northern State Mental Hospital."

Chalmers sat erect in his chair. He knew where that was; on the other side of the mountains, in the one part of the state completely untouched by the H-bombs of the Thirty Days' War. Why, the town outside which the hospital stood had been a military headquarters during the period immediately after the bombings, and the center from which all the rescue work in the state had been directed.

"And you thought you could commit me to Northern State!" he demanded, laughing scornfully, and this time he didn't try to make the laugh sound natural and unaffected. "You—confine *me*, anywhere? Confine a poor old history professor's body, yes, but that isn't me. I'm universal; I exist in all space-time. When this old body I'm wearing now was writing that book on the French Revolution, I was in Paris, watching it happen, from the fall of the Bastile to the Ninth Thermidor. I was in Basra, and saw that crazed tool of the Axis shoot down Khalid ib'n Hussein—and the professor talked about it a month before it happened. I have seen empires rise and stretch from star to star across the Galaxy, and crumble and fall. I have seen..."

Doctor Hauserman had gotten his pen out of his pocket and was signing the commitment form with one hand; with the other, he pressed a button on the desk. A door at the rear opened, and a large young man in a white jacket entered.

"You'll have to go away for a while, Professor," Hauserman was telling him, much later, after he had allowed himself to become calm again. "For how long, I don't know. Maybe a year or so."

"You mean to Northern State Mental?"

"Well... Yes, Professor. You've had a bad crack-up. I don't suppose you realize how bad. You've been working too hard; harder than your nervous system could stand. It's been too much for you."

"You mean, I'm nuts?"

"Please, Professor. I deplore that sort of terminology. You've had a severe psychological breakdown..."

"Will I be able to have books, and papers, and work a little? I couldn't bear the prospect of complete idleness."

"That would be all right, if you didn't work too hard."

"And could I say good-bye to some of my friends?"

Hauserman nodded and asked, "Who?"

"Well, Professor Pottgeiter..."

"He's outside now. He was inquiring about you."

"And Stanly Weill, my attorney. Not business; just to say good-bye."

"Oh, I'm sorry, Professor. He's not in town, now. He left almost immediately after...after..."

"After he found out I was crazy for sure? Where'd he go?"

"To Reno; he took the plane at five o'clock."

Weill wouldn't have believed, anyhow; no use trying to blame himself for that. But he was as sure that he would never see Stanly Weill alive again as he was that the next morning the sun would rise. He nodded impassively.

"Sorry he couldn't stay. Can I see Max Pottgeiter alone?"

"Yes, of course, Professor."

Old Pottgeiter came in, his face anguished. "Ed! It isn't true," he stammered. "I won't believe that it's true."

"What, Max?"

"That you're crazy. Nobody can make me believe that."

He put his hand on the old man's shoulder. "Confidentially, Max, neither do I. But don't tell anybody I'm not. It's a secret."

Pottgeiter looked troubled. For a moment, he seemed to be wondering if he mightn't be wrong and Hauserman and Whitburn and the others right.

"Max, do you believe in me?" he asked. "Do you believe that I knew about Khalid's assassination a month before it happened?"

"It's a horribly hard thing to believe," Pottgeiter admitted. "But, dammit, Ed, you did! I know, medieval history is full of stories about prophecies being fulfilled. I always thought those stories were just legends that grew up after the event. And, of course, he's about a century late for me, but there was Nostradamus. Maybe those old prophecies weren't just *ex post facto* legends, after all. Yes. After Khalid, I'll believe that."

"All right. I'm saying, now, that in a few days there'll be a bad explosion at Reno, Nevada. Watch the papers and the telecast for it. If it happens, that ought to prove it. And you remember what I told you about the Turks annexing Syria and Lebanon?" The old man nodded. "When that happens, get away from Blanley. Come up to the town where Northern State Mental Hospital is, and get yourself a place to live, and stay there. And try to bring Marjorie Fenner along with you. Will you do that, Max?"

"If you say so." His eyes widened. "Something bad's going to happen here?"

"Yes, Max. Something very bad. You promise me you will?"

"Of course, Ed. You know, you're the only friend I have around here. You and Marjorie. I'll come, and bring her along."

"Here's the key to my apartment." He got it from his pocket and gave it to Pottgeiter, with instructions. "Everything in the filing cabinet on the left of my desk. And don't let anybody else see any of it. Keep it safe for me."

The large young man in the white coat entered.

THE END

If you've enjoyed this book, you will not want to miss these terrific titles…

ARMCHAIR SCI-FI & HORROR DOUBLE NOVELS, $12.95 each

D-51　**A GOD NAMED SMITH** by Henry Slesar
　　　WORLDS OF THE IMPERIUM by Keith Laumer

D-52　**CRAIG'S BOOK** by Don Wilcox
　　　EDGE OF THE KNIFE by H. Beam Piper

D-53　**THE SHINING CITY** by Rena M. Vale
　　　THE RED PLANET by Russ Winterbotham

D-54　**THE MAN WHO LIVED TWICE** by Rog Phillips
　　　VALLEY OF THE CROEN by Lee Tarbell

D-55　**OPERATION DISASTER** by Milton Lesser
　　　LAND OF THE DAMNED by Berkeley Livingston

D-56　**CAPTIVE OF THE CENTAURIANESS** by Poul Anderson
　　　A PRINCESS OF MARS by Edgar Rice Burroughs

D-57　**THE NON-STATISTICAL MAN** by Raymond F. Jones
　　　MISSION FROM MARS by Rick Conroy

D-58　**INTRUDERS FROM THE STARS** by Ross Rocklynne
　　　FLIGHT OF THE STARLING by Chester S. Geier

D-59　**COSMIC SABOTEUR** by Frank M. Robinson
　　　LOOK TO THE STARS by Willard Hawkins

D-60　**THE MOON IS HELL!** by John W. Campbell, Jr.
　　　THE GREEN WORLD by Hal Clement

ARMCHAIR SCIENCE FICTION CLASSICS, $12.95 each

C-16　**THE SHAVER MYSTERY, Book Three**
　　　by Richard S. Shaver

C-17　**THE GIRLS FROM PLANET 5**
　　　by Richard Wilson

C-18　**THE FOURTH "R"**
　　　by George O. Smith

ARMCHAIR SCIENCE FICTION & HORROR GEMS SERIES, $12.95 each

G-5　**SCIENCE FICTION GEMS, Vol. Three**
　　　C. M. Kornbluth and others

G-6　**HORROR GEMS, Vol. Three**
　　　August Derleth and others

If you've enjoyed this book, you will not want to miss these terrific titles...

ARMCHAIR SCI-FI & HORROR DOUBLE NOVELS, $12.95 each

D-11   **PERIL OF THE STARMEN** by Kris Neville
THE STRANGE INVASION by Murray Leinster

D-12   **THE STAR LORD** by Boyd Ellanby
CAPTIVES OF THE FLAME by Samuel R. Delaney

D-13   **MEN OF THE MORNING STAR** by Edmund Hamilton
PLANET FOR PLUNDER by Hal Clement and Sam Merwin, Jr.

D-14   **ICE CITY OF THE GORGON** by Chester S. Geier and Richard Shaver
WHEN THE WORLD TOTTERED by Lester Del Rey

D-15   **WORLDS WITHOUT END** by Clifford D. Simak
THE LAVENDER VINE OF DEATH by Don Wilcox

D-16   **SHADOW ON THE MOON** by Joe Gibson
ARMAGEDDON EARTH by Geoff St. Reynard

D-17   **THE GIRL WHO LOVED DEATH** by Paul W. Fairman
SLAVE PLANET by Laurence M. Janifer

D-18   **SECOND CHANCE** by J. F. Bone
MISSION TO A DISTANT STAR by Frank Belknap Long

D-19   **THE SYNDIC** by C. M. Kornbluth
FLIGHT TO FOREVER by Poul Anderson

D-20   **SOMEWHERE I'LL FIND YOU** by Milton Lesser
THE TIME ARMADA by Fox B. Holden

ARMCHAIR SCIENCE FICTION CLASSICS, $12.95 each

C-4   **CORPUS EARTHLING**
by Louis Charbonneau

C-5   **THE TIME DISSOLVER**
by Jerry Sohl

C-6   **WEST OF THE SUN**
by Edgar Pangborn

ARMCHAIR SCIENCE FICTION & HORROR GEMS SERIES, $12.95 each

G-1   **SCIENCE FICTION GEMS, Vol. One**
Isaac Asimov and others

G-2   **HORROR GEMS, Vol. One**
Carl Jacobi and others

If you've enjoyed this book, you will not want to miss these terrific titles…

ARMCHAIR SCI-FI, FANTASY, & HORROR DOUBLE NOVELS, $12.95 each

D-21 **EMPIRE OF EVIL** by Robert Arnette
THE SIGN OF THE TIGER by Alan E. Nourse & J. A. Meyer

D-22 **OPERATION SQUARE PEG** by Frank Belknap Long
ENCHANTRESS OF VENUS by Leigh Brackett

D-23 **THE LIFE WATCH** by Lester Del Rey
CREATURES OF THE ABYSS by Murray Leinster

D-24 **LEGION OF LAZARUS** by Edmond Hamilton
STAR HUNTER by Andre Norton

D-25 **EMPIRE OF WOMEN** by John Fletcher
ONE OF OUR CITIES IS MISSING by Irving Cox

D-26 **THE WRONG SIDE OF PARADISE** by Raymond F. Jones
THE INVOLUNTARY IMMORTALS by Rog Phillips

D-27 **EARTH QUARTER** by Damon Knight
ENVOY TO NEW WORLDS by Keith Laumer

D-28 **SLAVES TO THE METAL HORDE** by Milton Lesser
HUNTERS OUT OF TIME by Joseph E. Kelleam

D-29 **RX JUPITER SAVE US** by Ward Moore
BEWARE THE USURPERS by Geoff St. Reynard

D-30 **SECRET OF THE SERPENT** by Don Wilcox
CRUSADE ACROSS THE VOID by Dwight V. Swain

ARMCHAIR SCIENCE FICTION CLASSICS, $12.95 each

C-7 **THE SHAVER MYSTERY, Book One**
by Richard S. Shaver

C-8 **THE SHAVER MYSTERY, Book Two**
by Richard S. Shaver

C-9 **MURDER IN SPACE** by David V. Reed
by David V. Reed

ARMCHAIR MASTERS OF SCIENCE FICTION SERIES, $16.95 each

M-3 **MASTERS OF SCIENCE FICTION, Vol. Three**
Robert Sheckley, "The Perfect Woman" and other tales

M-4 **MASTERS OF SCIENCE FICTION, Vol. Four**
Mack Reynolds, "Stowaway" and other tales

If you've enjoyed this book, you will not want to miss these terrific titles...

ARMCHAIR SCI-FI, FANTASY, & HORROR DOUBLE NOVELS, $12.95 each

D-41   **FULL CYCLE** by Clifford D. Simak
             IT WAS THE DAY OF THE ROBOT by Frank Belknap Long

D-42   **THIS CROWDED EARTH** by Robert Bloch
             REIGN OF THE TELEPUPPETS by Daniel Galouye

D-43   **THE CRISPIN AFFAIR** by Jack Sharkey
             THE RED HELL OF JUPITER by Paul Ernst

D-44   **PLANET OF DREAD** by Dwight V. Swain
             WE THE MACHINE by Gerald Vance

D-45   **THE STAR HUNTER** by Edmond Hamilton
             THE ALIEN by Raymond F. Jones

D-46   **WORLD OF IF** by Rog Phillips
             SLAVE RAIDERS FROM MERCURY by Don Wilcox

D-47   **THE ULTIMATE PERIL** by Robert Abernathy
             PLANET OF SHAME by Bruce Elliot

D-48   **THE FLYING EYES** by J. Hunter Holly
             SOME FABULOUS YONDER by Phillip Jose Farmer

D-49   **THE COSMIC BUNGLARS** by Geoff St. Reynard
             THE BUTTONED SKY by Geoff St. Reynard

D-50   **TYRANTS OF TIME** by Milton Lesser
             PARIAH PLANET by Murray Leinster

ARMCHAIR SCIENCE FICTION CLASSICS, $12.95 each

C-13   **SUNKEN WORLD**
             by Stanton A. Coblentz

C-14   **THE LAST VIAL**
             by Sam McClatchie, M. D.

C-15   **WE WHO SURVIVED (THE FIFTH ICE AGE)**
             by Sterling Noel

ARMCHAIR MASTERS OF SCIENCE FICTION SERIES, $16.95 each

MS-5   **MASTERS OF SCIENCE FICTION, Vol. Five**
             Winston K. Marks—Test Colony and other tales

MS-6   **MASTERS OF SCIENCE FICTION, Vol. Six**
             Fritz Leiber—Deadly Moon and other tales